Charles King

A Trooper Galahad

Charles King

A Trooper Galahad

ISBN/EAN: 9783743348790

Manufactured in Europe, USA, Canada, Australia, Japa

Cover: Foto ©Andreas Hilbeck / pixelio.de

Manufactured and distributed by brebook publishing software (www.brebook.com)

Charles King

A Trooper Galahad

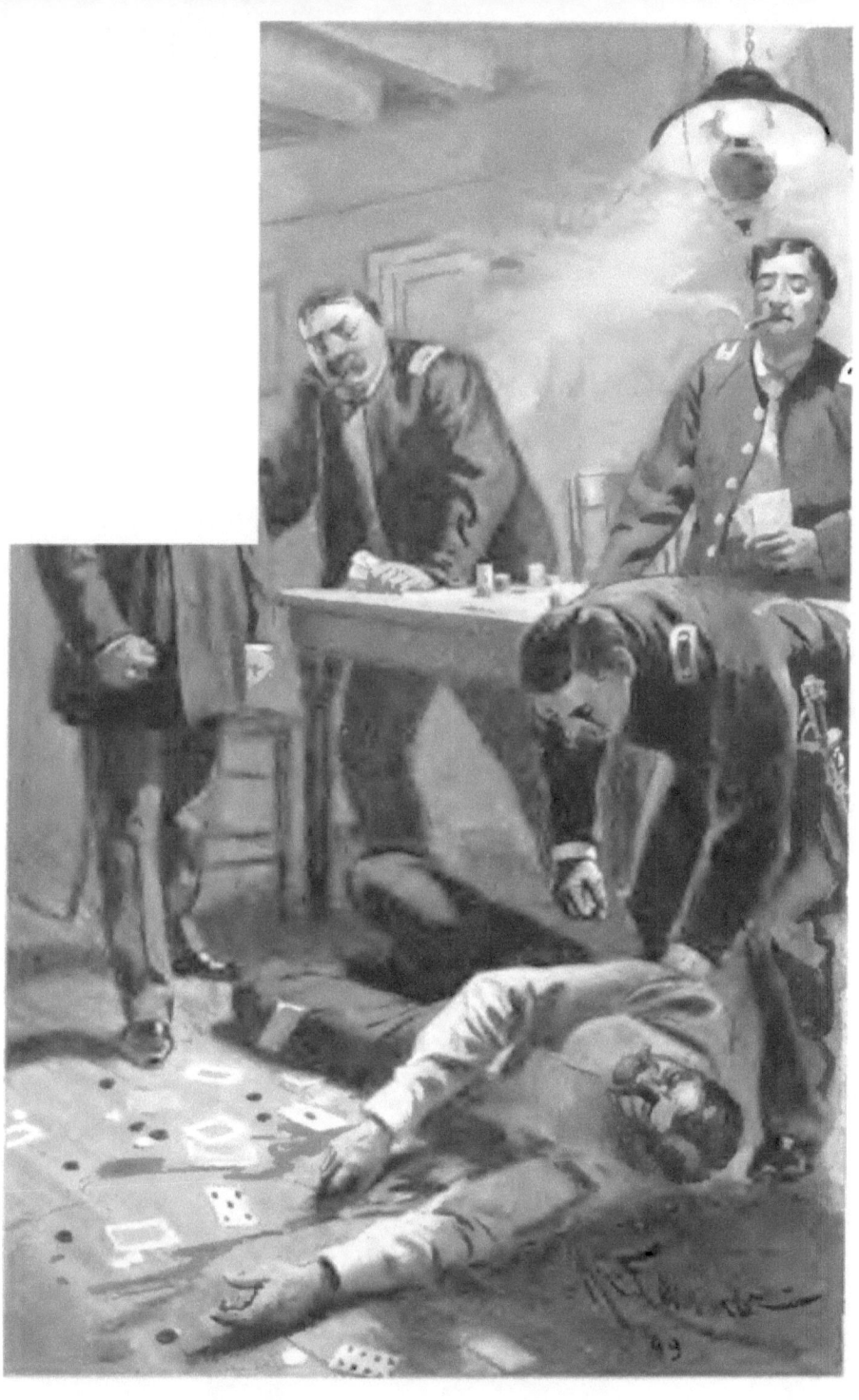

" Felling him like an ox."

A TROOPER GALAHAD

BY

CAPTAIN CHARLES KING, U.S.A.

AUTHOR OF

"THE COLONEL'S DAUGHTER," "MARION'S FAITH," "CAPTAIN BLAKE,"
"UNDER FIRE," "FROM SCHOOL TO BATTLE-FIELD," ETC.

PHILADELPHIA
J. B. LIPPINCOTT COMPANY
1899

A TROOPER GALAHAD

★ ★ ★

CHAPTER I.

"Life is full of ups and downs," mused the colonel, as he laid on the littered desk before him an official communication just received from Department Head-Quarters, "especially army life,—and more especially army life in Texas."

"Now, what are you philosophizing about?" asked his second in command, a burly major, glancing over the top of the latest home paper, three weeks old that day.

"D'ye remember Pigott, that little cad that was court-martialled at San Antonio in '68 for quintuplicating his pay accounts? He married the widow of old Alamo Hendrix that winter. He's worth half a million to-day, is running for Congress, and will probably be on the military committee next year, while here's Lawrence, who was judge advocate of the court that tried him, gone all to smash." And the veteran officer commanding the —th Infantry and the big post at Fort Worth glanced warily along into the adjoin-

3

ing office, where a clerk was assorting the papers
on the adjutant's desk.

"It's the saddest case I ever heard of," said
Major Brooks, tossing aside the *Toledo Blade* and
tripping up over his own, which he had thought-
fully propped between his legs as he took his seat
and thoughtlessly ignored as he left it. "Damn
that sabre,—and the service generally!" he
growled, as he recovered his balance and tramped
to the window. "I'd almost be willing to quit it
as Pigott did if I could see my way to a moderate
competence anywhere out of it. Lawrence was
as good a soldier as we had in the 12th, and, yet,
what can you do or say? The mischief's done."
And, beating the devil's tattoo on the window,
the major stood gloomily gazing out over the
parade.

"It isn't Lawrence himself I'm so—— Orderly, shut that door!" cried the chief, whirling
around in his chair, "and tell those clerks I want
it kept shut until the adjutant comes; and you
stay out on the porch.—It isn't Lawrence I'm so
sorely troubled about, Brooks. He has ability,
and could pick up and do well eventually, but
he's utterly discouraged and swamped. What's
to become, though, of that poor child Ada and his
little boy?"

"God knows," said Brooks, sadly. "I've got

five of my own to look after, and you've got four.
No use talking of adopting them, even if Lawrence would listen; and he never would listen
to anything or anybody—they tell me," he added,
after a minute's reflection. "I don't know it myself. It's what Buxton and Canker and some of
those fellows told me on the Republican last summer. I hadn't seen him since Gettysburg until
we met here."

"Buxton and Canker be—exterminated!" said
the colonel, hotly. "I never met Buxton, and
never want to. As for Canker, by gad, there's
another absurdity. They put him in the cavalry
because consolidation left no room for him with
us. What do you suppose they'll do with him in
the —th?"

"The Lord knows, as I said before. He never
rode anything but a hobby in his life. I don't
wonder Lawrence couldn't tolerate preaching
from him. But what I don't understand is, who
made the allegation. What's his offence? Every
one knows that he's in debt and trouble, and that
he's had hard lines and nothing else ever since the
war, but the court acquitted him of all blame in
that money business——"

"And now to make room for fellows with
friends at court," burst in the colonel, wrathfully,
"he and other poor devils with nothing but a

fighting record and a family to provide for are
turned loose on a year's pay, which they're to
have after things straighten out as to their accounts with the government.   Now just look at
Lawrence! Ordnance and quartermaster's stores
hopelessly boggled——"

"Hush!" interrupted Brooks, starting back
from the window.   "Here he is now."

Assembly of the guard details had sounded a
few moments before, and all over the sunshiny
parade on its westward side, in front of the
various barracks, little squads of soldiers armed
and in full uniform were standing awaiting the
next signal, while the porches of the low wooden
buildings beyond were dotted with groups of
comrades, lazily looking on.   Out on the greensward, broad and level, crisscrossed with gravel
walks, the band had taken its station, marshalled
by the tall drum-major in his huge bear-skin
shako.   From the lofty flag-staff in the centre of
the parade the national colors were fluttering in
the mountain breeze that stole down from the
snowy peaks hemming the view to the northwest
and stirred the leaves of the cottonwoods and the
drooping branches of the willows in the bed of
the rushing stream sweeping by the southern
limits of the garrison.   Within the enclosure,
sacred to military use, it was all the same old

familiar picture, the stereotyped fashion of the
frontier fort of the earliest '70s,—dull-hued barracks on one side or on two, dull-hued, broad-
porched cottages—the officers' quarters—on
another, dull-hued offices, storehouses, corral
walls, scattered about the outskirts, a dull-hued,
sombre earth on every side; sombre sweeping
prairie beyond, spanned by pallid sky or snow-
tipped mountains; a twisting, winding road or
two, entering the post on one front, issuing at
the other, and tapering off in sinuous curves
until lost in the distance; a few scattered ranches
in the stream valley; a collection of sheds,
shanties, and hovels surrounding a bustling establishment known as the store, down by the
ford,—the centre of civilization, apparently, for
thither trended every roadway, path, track, or
trail visible to the naked eye. Here in front of
the office a solitary cavalry horse was tethered.
Yonder at the sutler's, early as it was in the day,
a dozen quadrupeds, mules, mustangs, or Indian
ponies, were blinking in the sunshine. Dogs in-
numerable sprawled in the sand. Bipeds lolled
lazily about or squatted on the steps on the edge
of the wooden porch, some in broad sombreros,
some in scalp-lock and blanket,—none in the garb
of civil life as seen in the nearest cities, and the
nearest was four or five hundred miles away.

Out on the parade were bits of lively color, the dresses of frolicsome children to the east, the stripes and facings of the cavalry and artillery at the west; for, by some odd freak of the fortunes of war, here, away out at Fort Worth, had come a crack light battery of the old army, which, with Brooks's battalion of the cavalry, and head-quarters' staff, band, and six companies of the —th Infantry, made up the garrison,—the biggest then maintained in the Department immortalized by Sheridan as only second choice to Sheol. It was the winter of '70 and '71, as black and dreary a time as ever the army knew, for Congress had telescoped forty-five regiments into half the number and blasted all hopes of promotion,—about the only thing the soldier has to live for.

And that wasn't the blackest thing about the business, by any means. The war had developed the fact that we had thousands of battalion commanders for whom the nation had no place in peace times, and scores of them, in the hope and promise of a life employment in an honorable profession, accepted the tender of lieutenancies in the regular army in '66, the war having broken up all their vocations at home, and now, having given four years more to the military service,— taken all those years out of their lives that might have been given to establishing themselves in business,—they were bidden to choose between voluntarily quitting the army with a bonus of a year's pay, and remaining with no hope of advancement. Most of them, despairing of finding employment in civil life, concluded to stay: so other methods of getting rid of them were devised, and, to the amaze of the army and the dismay of the victims, a big list was published of officers "rendered supernumerary" and summarily discharged. And this was how it happened that a gallant, brilliant, and glad-hearted fellow, the favorite staff officer of a glorious corps commander who fell at the head of his men after three years of equally glorious service, found himself in far-away Texas this blackest of black Fridays, suddenly turned loose on the world and without hope or home.

Cruel was no word for it. Entering the army before the war, one of the few gifted civilians commissioned because they loved the service and then had friends to back them, Edgar Lawrence had joined the cavalry in Texas, where the first thing he did was to fall heels over head in love with his captain's daughter, and a runaway match resulted. Poor Kitty Tyrrell! Poor Ned Lawrence! Two more unpractical people never lived. She was an army girl with aspirations, much sweetness, and little sense. He was a whole-

souled, generous, lavish fellow. Both were extravagant, she particularly so. They were sorely
in debt when the war broke out, and he, instead
of going in for the volunteers, was induced to become aide-de-camp to his old colonel, who passed
him on to another when he retired; and when the
war was half over Lawrence was only a captain
of staff, and captain he came out at the close.
Brevets of course he had, but what are brevets
but empty title? What profiteth it a man to be
called colonel if he have only the pay of a sub?
Hundreds of men who eagerly sought his aid or
influence during the war "held over him" at the
end of it. Another general took him on his staff
as aide-de-camp, where Lawrence was invaluable.
Kitty dearly loved city life, parties, balls, operas,
and theatres; but Lawrence grew lined and gray
with care and worry. The general went the way
of all flesh, and Lawrence to Texas, unable to get
another staff billet. They set him at court-martial duty at San Antonio for several months, for
Texas furnished culprits by the score in the days
that followed the war, and many an unpromising
army career was cut short by the tribunal of
which Captain and Brevet Lieutenant-Colonel
Lawrence was judge advocate; but all the time
he had a skeleton in his own closet that by and
by rattled its way out. Time was in the war days

when many of the men of the head-quarters escort banked their money with the beloved and popular aide. He had nearly twelve hundred dollars when the long columns probed the Wilderness in '64. It was still with him when he was suddenly sent back to Washington with the body of his beloved chief, but every cent was gone before he got there, stolen from him on the steamer from Acquia Creek, and never a trace was found of it thereafter. For years he was paying that off, making it good in driblets, but while he was serving faithfully in Texas, commanding a scout that took him miles and miles away over the Llano Estacado, there were inimical souls who worked the story of his indebtedness to enlisted men for all it was worth, and, aided by the complaints of some of their number, to his grievous disadvantage. He came home from a brilliant dash after the Kiowas to find himself complimented in orders and confronted by charges in one and the same breath. The court acquitted him of the charges and "cut" his accusers, but the shame and humiliation of it all seemed to prey upon his spirits; and then Kitty Tyrrell died.

"If that had only happened years before," said the colonel, "it would have been far better for Lawrence, for she conscientiously believed her-

self the best wife in the world, and spent every
cent of his income in dressing up to her concep-
tion of the character." Once the most dashing
and debonair of captains, poor Ned ran down at
the heel and seemed unable to rally. New commanders came to the department, to his regiment,
and new officials to the War Office,—men "who
knew not Joseph;" and when the drag-net was cast
into the whirlpool of army names and army repu-
tations, it was set for scandal, not for services,
and the old story of those unpaid hundreds was
enmeshed and served up seasoned with the latest
spice obtainable from the dealers rebuked of that
original court. And, lo! when the list of victims
reached Fort Worth in the reorganization days,
old Frazier, the colonel, burst into a string of
anathemas, and more than one good woman into
a passion of tears, for poor Ned Lawrence, at that
moment long days' marches away towards the Rio
Bravo, was declared supernumerary and mustered
out of the service of the United States with one
year's pay,—pay which he could not hope to get
until every government account was satisfactorily
straightened, and this, too, at a time when the
desertion of one sergeant and the death of another revealed the fact that his storehouses had
been systematically robbed and that he was hopelessly short in many a costly item charged against

him. That heartless order was a month old when the stricken soldier reached his post, and then and there for the first time learned his fate.

Yes, they had tried to break it to him. Letters full of sympathy were written and sent by couriers far to the north; others took them on the Concho trail. Brooks and Frazier both wrote to San Antonio messages thence to be wired to Washington imploring reconsideration; but the deed was done. Astute advisers of the War Secretary clinched the matter by the prompt renomination of others to fill the vacancies just created, and once these were confirmed by the Senate there could be no appeal. The detachment led by Brevet Lieutenant-Colonel Lawrence, so later said the Texas papers, had covered itself with glory, but in its pursuit of the fleeing Indians it had gone far to the northeast and so came home by a route no man had dreamed of, and Lawrence, spurring eagerly ahead, rode in at night to fold his motherless little ones to his heart, and found loving army women aiding their faithful old nurse in ministering to them, but read disaster in the tearful eyes and faltering words that welcomed him.

Then he was ill a fortnight, and then he had to go. He could not, would not believe the order final. He clung to the hope that he would find at Washington a dozen men who knew his war

record, who could remember his gallant services
in a dozen battles, his popularity and prominence
in the Army of the Potomac. Everybody knows
the favorite aide-de-camp of a corps commander
when colonels go begging for recognition, and
everybody has a cheery, cordial word for him so
long as he and his general live and serve together.
But that proves nothing when the general is gone.
Colonels who eagerly welcomed and shook hands
with the aide-de-camp and talked confidentially
with him about other colonels in days when he
rode long hours by his general's side, later passed
him by with scant notice, and "always thought
him a much overrated man." Right here at Fort
Worth were fellows who, six or seven years before, would have given a month's pay to win Ned
Lawrence's influence in their behalf,—for, like
"Perfect" Bliss of the Mexican war days, Lawrence was believed to write his general's de-
spatches and reports,—but who now shrank uneasily out of his way for fear that he should ask
a favor.

Even Brooks, who liked and had spoken for
him, drew back from the window when with slow,
heavy steps the sad-faced, haggard man came
slowly along the porch. The orderly sprang up
and stood at salute just as adjutant's call sounded,
and the band pealed forth its merry, spirited

music. For a moment the new-comer turned and
glanced back over the parade, now dotted with
little details all marching out to the line where
stood the sergeant-major; then he turned, entered the building, and paused with hopeless eyes
and pallid, careworn features at the office doorway. His old single-breasted captain's frock-coat,
with its tarnished silver leaves at the shoulders,
hung loosely about his shrunken form. The
trousers, with their narrow welt of yellow at the
seam, looked far too big for him. His forage-cap,
still natty in shape, was old and worn. His chin
and cheeks bristled with a stubbly grayish beard.
All the old alert manner was gone. The once
bright eyes were bleary and dull. Neighbors said
that poor Ned had been drinking deep of the contents of a demijohn a sympathetic soul had sent
him, and half an eye could tell that his lip was
tremulous. The colonel arose and held out his
hand.

"Come in, Lawrence, old fellow, and tell me
what I can do for you." He spoke kindly, and
Brooks, too, turned towards the desolate man.

"You've done—all you could—both of you.
God bless you!" was the faltering answer. "I've
come to say I start at once. I'm going right to
Washington to have this straightened out. I
want to thank you, colonel, and you too, Brooks,

for all your willing help. I'll try to show my appreciation of it when I get back."

"But Ada and little Jim, Lawrence; surely they're not ready for that long journey yet," said Frazier, thinking sorrowfully of what his wife had told him only the day before,—that they had no decent winter clothing to their names.

"It's all right. Old Mammy stays right here with them. She has taken care of them, you know, ever since my poor wife died. I can keep my old quarters a month, can't I?" he queried, with a quivering smile. "Even if the order isn't revoked, it would be a month or more before any one could come to take my place. Mrs. Blythe will look after the children day and night."

Frazier turned appealingly to Brooks, who shook his head and refused to speak, and so the colonel had to.

"Lawrence, God knows I hate to say one word of discouragement, but I fear—I fear you'd better wait till next week's stage and take those poor little folks with you. I've watched this thing. I know how a dozen good fellows, confident as yourself, have gone on to Washington and found it all useless."

"It can't be useless, sir," burst in the captain, impetuously. "Truth is truth and must prevail. If after all my years of service I can find no friends in the War Office, then life is a lie and a sham. Senator Hall writes me that he will leave no stone unturned. No, colonel, I take the stage at noon to-day. Will you let Winn ride with me as far as Castle Peak? I've got to run down and see Fuller now."

"Winn can go with you, certainly; but indeed, Lawrence, I shall have to see you again about this."

"I'll stop on the way back," said Lawrence, nervously. "Fuller promised to see me before he went out to his ranch." And hastily the captain turned away.

For a moment the two seniors stood there silently gazing into each other's eyes. "What can one do or say?" asked the colonel, at last. "I suppose Fuller is going to let him have money for the trip. He can afford to, God knows, after all he's made out of this garrison. But the question is, ought I not to make poor Lawrence understand that it's a gone case? He is legally out already. His successor is on his way here. I got the letter this morning."

"On his way here? Who is he?" queried the major, in sudden interest. "They didn't know when Stone came through San Antonio ten days ago."

"Man named Barclay; just got his captaincy

in the 30th,—but was consolidated out of that, of course."

"Barclay—Barclay, you say?" ejaculated the major, in excitement. "Well, of all the———"

"Of all the what?" demanded the colonel, impatiently. "Nothing wrong with him, I hope."

"Wrong? No, or they wouldn't have dubbed him Galahad. But, talk about ups and downs in Texas, this beats all. Does Winn know?"

"I don't know that any one knows but you and me," answered the veteran, half testily. "What's amiss? What has Winn to do with it?"

"Blood and blue blazes! Why, of course you couldn't know. Three years ago Barclay believed himself engaged to a girl, and she threw him over for Winn, and now we'll have all three of them right here at Worth."

CHAPTER II.

In spite of what Colonel Frazier could say, Captain Lawrence had gone the long and devious journey to Washington. Those were the days when the lumbering stage-coach once a week, or a rattling ambulance, bore our army travellers from the far frontier to San Antonio. Another trundled and bumped them away to the Gulf. A Morgan Line steamer picked them up and tossed and rolled with them to the mouth of the Mississippi and unloaded them at New Orleans, whence by dusty railway journey of forty-eight hours or more they could hope to reach the North. The parting between Lawrence and his tall slip of a daughter and boisterous little Jimmy was something women wept over in telling or hearing, for only two looked on, well-nigh blinded,—Mrs. Blythe, who had been devoted to their mother, and old "Mammy," who was devoted to them all. A month had rolled by, and the letters that came from Lawrence from San Antonio and Indianola and New Orleans had been read by sympathizing friends to the children. Then all awaited the news from Washington. Every one knew he

19

would wire to Department Head-Quarters the
moment the case was settled in his favor; but the
days went by without other tidings, and the
croakers who had predicted ill success were
mournfully happy. February passed, March was
ushered in; orders came transferring certain por-
tions of Frazier's big command, and certain new
officers began to arrive to fill the three or four
vacancies existing, but the new captain of Troop
"D" of the cavalry had not yet appeared. His
fame, however, had preceded him, and all Fort
Worth was agog to meet him. Brooks knew but
a modest bit of his story, and what he knew he
kept from every man but Frazier, yet had had to
tell his wife. The Winns were silent on the subject. Winn himself was a man of few intimates,
—a young first lieutenant of cavalry,—and the
tie that bound him to Lawrence was the fact that
he and Kitty Tyrrell were first-cousins, their
mothers sisters, and Winn, a tall, athletic, slender
fellow, frank, buoyant, handsome, and connected
with some of the best names in the old army, was
one of the swells of his class at the Point and the
beau among all the young officers the summer of
his graduation,—the summer that Laura Waite,
engaged to Brevet Captain Galbraith Barclay of
the Infantry, came from the West to visit relatives at that enchanting spot, spent just six weeks

there, and, after writing letters all one month to
close her absent lover's eyes, wound up by writing
one that opened them. She was a beautiful girl
then; she was a lovely-looking woman now, but
the bloom was gone. The brilliant eyes were
often clouded, for Harry Winn was "his aunt
Kitty all over," said many a man who knew them
both. Their name was impecuniosity. That
Mrs. Winn could tell much about the coming
captain letters from other regiments informed
more than one bright woman at Worth; but that
the young matron would tell next to nothing,
more than one woman, bright or blundering, discovered on inquiry. Only one officer now at the
post had ever served with Barclay, and that was
Brooks, who became tongue-tied so soon as it was
settled beyond peradventure that Captain Galbraith Barclay from the unassigned list had been
gazetted to the 12th Cavalry, Troop "D," *vice*
Lawrence, honorably discharged. But Brooks
had letters, so had Frazier, from old officers who
had served with the transferred man. Some of
these letters referred to him in terms of admiration, while another spoke of him unhesitatingly as
"more kinds of a damned fool" than the writer
had ever met. Verily, various men have various
minds.

Presently, however, there came a man who

could tell lots about Barclay, whether he knew
anything or not, and that was one of the new
transfers, Lieutenant Hodge by title and name.
Hodge said he had served with the 30th along
the Union Pacific, and had met Barclay often.
In his original regiment Mr. Hodge had been regarded as a very monotonous sort of man, a fellow
who bored his hearers to death, and the contrast
between his reception in social circles in the regiment he had left, and that accorded him here at
Worth so soon as it was learned that he knew
Barclay, inspired Mr. Hodge to say that *these* people were worth knowing; they had some life and
intelligence about them.   The gang he had left
in Wyoming were a stupid lot of owls by com-
parison.   For a week Hodge was invited to dinner by family after family, and people dropped
in to spend the evening where he happened to be,
for Hodge held the floor and talked for hours
about Barclay, and what he had to tell was interesting indeed; so much so, said Brooks, that some
of it was probably a preposterous lie.   To begin
with, said Hodge, Captain Barclay was rich, very
rich, fabulously rich, perhaps; nobody knew how
rich, and nobody would have known he was rich
at all, judging from the simplicity and strict
economy of his life.   In fact, it was this simplicity
and strict economy that had given rise to the belief

that existed for a year or two after he joined the
30th that he was hampered either with debts or
with dependent relatives. Relatives they knew he
had, because sisters sent their boys to visit him at
Sanders, and he took them hunting, fishing, etc.;
from these ingenuous nephews the ladies learned
of others, nephews, nieces, sisters, cousins, aunts,
who wrote long letters to Uncle Gal, and the mail
orderly said he left more letters at Captain Barclay's quarters than at anybody's else. So Fort
Sanders dropped the theory of debts and adopted
that of dependants, and that held good for the
first year of his service with them. He had joined
from the volunteers, where he had risen to the
grade of major. He was "pious," said Hodge,—
wouldn't drink, smoke, chew, play cards, or swear,
—thought they ought to have services on Sunday. He left the roistering bachelors' mess soon
after his reaching the post, and had ever since
kept house, his cook and housemaid being one old
darky whom he had "accumulated" in the South
during the war,—a darky who had been well-
taught in the household of his old master, and
who became extravagantly attached to the new.
Hannibal could cook, wait at table, and tend door
to perfection, but he had to learn the duties of
second girl when his master joined the 30th in
far Wyoming, and that was the only time a

breach was threatened. Hannibal's dignity was hurt. He had been body-servant in the ante-bellum days, butler, cook, coachman, and hostler, but had never done such chores as Marse Barclay told him would fall to his lot when that reticent officer set up his modest establishment. Hannibal sulked three days, and even talked of leaving. The lieutenant counted out a goodly sum, all Hannibal's own, and told him that he would find the balance banked in his name in the distant East whenever he chose to quit; then Hannibal broke down, and was speedily broken in. All this had Hodge heard when the dames of Sanders and those of Steele or Russell were comparing notes and picnicking together along that then new wonder of the world, the Union Pacific. But all this was only preliminary to what came later.

Little detachments, horse and foot, were scattered all over the line of the brand-new railway while it was being built; every now and then the Indians jumped their camps and working-parties, and in the late fall of '67 Barclay had a stiff and plucky fight with a band of Sioux; he was severely wounded, but beat them off, and was sent East to recuperate. Now came particulars Hodge could not give, but that letters could and did. It was while Barclay was convalescing at Omaha Barracks that he met Miss Laura Waite,—a beautiful girl and a garrison belle. She was ten years his junior. This was her first winter in army society. She had spent her girl years at school, and now was having "simply a heavenly time," if her letters could be believed. Her father was a field officer of cavalry with rather a solemn way of looking at life, and her mother was said to be the explanation of much of his solemnity,—she being as volatile as he was staid. She too had been a beauty, and believed that beauty a permanent fixture. But Laura was fresh and fair, sweet and winsome, light-hearted and joyous, and the father for a time took more pride in her than he did in his sons. Major Waite was in command of the cantonment from which the relief party was sent when the news came that Barclay and his little detachment were "corralled." Major Waite became enthusiastic over the details of the cool, courageous, brainy defence made by the young officer against tremendous odds, covered him with all manner of thoughtful care and attention when he was brought into the cantonment, then, when the winter soon set in and the camp broke up, and Waite went back to Omaha Barracks, he took Barclay with him to his house instead of the hospital, and the rest followed as the night the day.

Barclay spent a month under the major's roof,

won his esteem and friendship, but left his heart in the daughter's hands. If ever a man devotedly loved a beautiful, winsome young girl, that man was Galbraith Barclay; if ever a girl's father approved of a man, that man was Barclay; and if ever a man had reason to hope that his suit would win favor in a father's eyes, that man was Barclay; yet it did not. Major Waite's reply to the modest yet most manful plea of Lieutenant Barclay to be permitted to pay his addresses to the major's daughter surprised every one to whom Mrs. Waite confided it, and they were not few. The old soldier begged of the younger not to think of it, at least just yet. But when it transpired that the younger had been most seriously thinking of it and could think of nothing else, then the major changed his tune and told him what he did not tell his wife; and that only became known through the father's own intemperate language long months after. He told Barclay he knew no man to whom he would rather intrust his daughter's happiness, but he feared, he believed, she was still too young to know her own mind, too young to see in Barclay what he saw, and he urged that the young officer should wait. But Barclay knew *his* own mind. He was able, he said, to provide for her in comfort either in or out of the army, which few possible aspirants could say. He would listen to no demur, and then at last the father said, "Try your fate if you will, but let there be no thought of marriage before she is twenty,—before she can have had opportunity of seeing something of the world and of other men,—not these young whippersnappers just joining us here."

It was a surprise to him that Laura should accept Mr. Barclay. She came to him, her father, all happy smiles and tears and blushes, and told him how proud and glad a girl she was, because she thought her lover the best and noblest man she ever dreamed of except her own dear old dad. For a time Waite took heart and hoped for the best, and believed her and her mother, as indeed they believed themselves; and when Barclay went back to Sanders at the end of January he was a very happy man, and Laura for a week a very lonely girl. Then youth, health, elasticity, vivacity, opportunity, all prevailed, and she began to take notice in very joyous fashion. She did not at all recognize the doctrine preached by certain mammas and certain other damsels, that she as an engaged girl should hold aloof now and give the other girls, not so pretty, a chance. The barracks were gay that winter: Laura danced with the gayest, and when Barclay got leave in April and came down for a fortnight he found himself

much in the way of two young gentlemen who
danced delightfully, a thing he could not do at
all. Yet he had sweet hours with his sweetheart,
and grew even more deeply in love, so beautiful
was she growing, and went back to Sanders a
second time thinking himself happiest of the
happy, or bound to be when, in the coming au-
tumn, he could claim her as his own. But Waite
was troubled. He was to take the field the 1st
of May; his troops would be in saddle and on
scout away to the west all summer long; his wife
and daughter were to spend those months at the
sea-shore and in shopping for the great event to
come in November. He had a long, earnest talk
with Barclay when once more the devoted fellow
came to see the lady of his love on the eve of her
departure for the East, but Barclay looked into
her radiant, uplifted eyes, and could not read the
shadow of coming events, of which she was as
ignorant as he. In May he led his men on the
march to the Big Horn, and in June she led with
Cadet Lieutenant Winn the german at the graduation hop at West Point. Then Winn was as-
signed to duty, as was the custom of the day, one
of two or three young graduates chosen as assistant instructors during the summer camp. He
had an hour to devote to drill each morning and
a dozen to devote to the girls, and Laura Waite,

with her lovely face and form, was the talk of
the brilliant throng of visitors that summer. She
and her mother returned to the Point as guests
of some old friends there stationed, a visit which
was not on the original programme at all. Winn
took the girl riding day after day, and to hops
week after week. The shopping for the wedding
went on betweentimes, and Winn even escorted
them to the city and took part in the shopping.
In fine, when November came, in spite of the
furious opposition of her father, in spite of his
refusal to attend the ceremony or to countenance
it in any way, Winn, *vice* Barclay, honorably discharged, appeared as groom, and bore his bride
away to a round of joyous festivities among army
friends in New Orleans and San Antonio before
their final exile to the far frontier. From that
day to this no line had ever come from the
angered and aging man, even when Laura's baby
girl was born. Funds he sent from time to time,
—he knew he'd have to do that, as he told her
mother and she told her friends,—and then, just
as more funds were much needed because of pressing claims of creditors whose bills had not been
paid from previous remittances, Winn being
much in the field and Laura becoming disburser
general in his absence, the major suddenly died,
leaving a small life insurance for his disconsolate

widow and nothing to speak of for his children.
They had sucked him dry during his busy life.

The Winns did not invite Mr. Hodge to dinner, and were not bidden to meet him.   Laura
was still in light mourning for her father, and
for days she really heard very little of Hodge's
revelations regarding her discarded Wyoming
lover.   It was through the nurse-girl, an old
soldier's daughter, that she first began to glean
the chaff of the stories flitting from house to
house, and to hear the exaggeration of Hodge's
romancings about Captain Barclay's wealth, for
that, after all, proved the most vividly interesting
of the travellers' tales he told.   Barclay proved
to be, said Hodge, an expert mineralogist and
geologist, and this was of value when a craze for
dabbling in mining stocks swept over Sanders.
Barclay, who lived so simply in garrison, was discovered (through a breach of confidence on the
part of the officiating clergyman, that well-nigh
led to another breach) to be the principal sub-
scriber to the mission church being built in
Laramie City.   It suddenly became known that
Barclay had a balance in the local bank and reserve funds at the East, whereupon promoters
and prospectors by the dozen called upon him at
the fort and strove to induce him to take stock in
their mines.   Nine out of ten were sent to the

right-about, even those who called his attention to
the fact that Colonel This and Major That were
large shareholders. One or two he gave ear to,
and later got leave of absence and visited their
distant claims. He was out prospecting, said
Hodge, half the time in the fall of '68. The
ventures of the other officers seemed to prove
prolific sources of assessments. The Lord only
knows how much fun and money the mine-owners
of those days got out of the army. But they
failed to impress the puritanical captain, and by
the summer of '69 they ceased to do business in
his neighborhood, for before sending good money
after bad, officers had taken to consulting Barclay, and many an honest fellow's hoarded savings
were spared to his wife and children, all through
Barclay's calm and patient exposition of the fal-
lacy of the "Company's" claims.

Then, said Hodge, when Channing, of the
27th, was killed by Red Cloud's band back of
Laramie Peak, and his heart-broken widow and
children were left penniless, somebody found the
money to send them all to their friends in New
England and to see them safely established there.
And when Porter's wife was taken so ill while he
was away up north of the Big Horn, and the doctor said that a trained nurse must be had in the
first place, there came one from far Chicago; and

later, after Porter reached the post, overjoyed to
find his beloved one slowly mending and so skilfully guarded, the doctors told him she must be
taken to the sea-shore or the South, and, though
every one at Sanders knew poor Porter had not a
penny, it was all arranged somehow, and Emily
Porter came back the next winter a rosy, bloom-
ing, happy wife. No one knew for certain that
all the needed money came from Barclay, but as
the Porters seemed to adore him from that time
on, and their baby boy was baptized Galbraith
Barclay, everybody had reason to believe it. If
Mrs. Winn ever wanted to experience the exhila-
ration of hearing what other people thought of
her, she had only, said Mr. Hodge in confidence,
to turn Mrs. Porter loose on that subject.

Then, too, said Hodge, there was Ordnance
Sergeant Murphy and his family, burned out one
winter's night with all their savings, and the old
man dreadfully scorched in trying to rescue his
strong box from the flames. It must have been
Barclay who looked after the mother and kids all
the time the old man was moaning in hospital.
They moved him into a newly furnished and comfortable shack inside of a fortnight, and the Mur-
phys had another saint on their domestic calendar,
despite the non-appearance of his name in the
voluminous records of their Church. All this and

more did Hodge tell of Barclay, as in duty bound, he said, after first telling what other fellows long said of him,—that he was close and mean, a prig, a namby-pamby (despite the way he fought Crow-Killer's warlike band), a wet blanket to garrison joys, etc., etc.; and yet they really couldn't tell why. He subscribed just as much to the hop fund, though he didn't hop,—to the supper fund, though he didn't sup,—to the mess fund for the entertainment of visiting officers, though he didn't drink,—to the dramatic fund, though he couldn't act,—to the garrison hunt, though they said he couldn't ride. But he declined to give one cent towards the deficiency bill that resulted when Sanders entertained Steele at an all-night symposium at the sutler's and opened case after case of champagne and smoked box after box of cigars. "It was a senseless, soulless proceeding," said he, with brutal frankness. "Half the money you drank or smoked up in six hours could have clothed and fed all the children in Sudstown for six months."

"Lord, but they were mad all through," said Hodge, when describing it. "There wasn't a name they didn't call him all that winter."

"And yet I hear," said Mrs. Tremaine, a woman Fort Worth loved and looked up to as the —th did to Mrs. Stannard, "that for a long time past they have called him Sir Galahad instead of Galbraith."

"Oh," said Hodge, "that's one of old Gleason's jokes. He said they called him 'Gal I had' when he went to Omaha and 'Gal I hadn't' when he got back,"—a statement which sent Major Brooks swearing *sotto voce* from the room.

"I don't know which I'd rather kick," said he, "Hodge or Gleason. I'd rejoice in Barclay's coming if it weren't—if Lawrence were only here, if Winn were only away."

CHAPTER III.

An unhappy man was Major Brooks that gloomy month of March. The news from Washington *via* Department Head-Quarters was most discouraging as to Lawrence. He was both looking and doing ill. It seemed to "break him all up," said a letter from a friend in the Adjutant-General's office, that so few could be found to urge the Secretary to do something for him. What could they do? was the answer. Admitting that Lawrence had been grievously wronged, "whose fault was it?" said the Secretary; "not mine." He had only acted on the information and recommendation of officers to whom this work had been intrusted. If they had erred, he should have been informed of it before. "How could you be informed," said the Senator who had championed the poor fellow's cause, "when you resorted to a system that would have shamed a Spaniard in the days of the Inquisition, or the Bourbons with their *lettres de cachet* and the Bastile?" No one dreamed that Lawrence was in danger until he was done to death, and so, out of money, out of clothes, out of hope, health, and courage, poor Ned was fretting his heart out, while tender women and loyal friends were keeping guard over his shabby army home and caring for his two motherless lambs away out on the far frontier, awaiting the day when he should be restored to them.

It did not come, nor did Lawrence. An old comrade of the Sixth Corps, a gallant volunteer brigade commander, then in prosperous circumstances at Washington, had given him the shelter of his home, only too gladly keeping him in rations and cigars, as he would have done in clothes and pocket-money, but he shook his head at whiskey. "For God's sake, Ned, and for your babies' sake, leave that alone. It can't help you. You never were a drinking man before. Don't drink now, or your nerve will give out utterly." This and more he urged and pleaded, but Lawrence's pride seemed crushed and his heart broken. Legal advisers told his friends at last that restoration was impossible: his place was filled. He had only one course left if he would listen to nothing but restoration to the army, and that was to accept a second lieutenancy and begin over again at the bottom of the list. They broached it to him, and he broke out into wild, derisive laughter. "Good God! do you mean that a man who has served fifteen years in the army,

fought all through the war and served as I have
served, must step down from the squadron captaincy to ride behind the boys just out of the
Point? be ranked out of quarters by my own son-
in-law the next thing I know! I'll see the army
in hell first," was his furious reply.

"No, Ned, not hell, but Texas. Take it; go
back to the line, and once you're back in the army
in any grade we'll legislate you up to the majority
you deserve: see if we don't."

But Lawrence had lost all faith in promises, or
in Congressional action. He turned in contempt
from the proposition, and in early April came the
tidings to San Antonio that he was desperately
ill.

Meanwhile Mr. Hodge had lost the *prestige* of
his first appearance at Worth, and fell into the
customary rut of the subaltern. People found him
as monotonous as did the martyrs of the Upper
Platte, and, from having been the most sought-
after of second lieutenants, he dropped back to
the plane of semi-obscurity. This was galling.
Hodge's stock in trade had been the facts or fa-
bles in his possession concerning the absent Captain Barclay, whose present whereabouts and
plans were shrouded in mystery. A rumor came
that he had decided not to join at all; that he
was in Washington striving to arrange a transfer;

that his assignment to the regiment and to the post where he must meet the woman who had jilted him for a cavalry subaltern was something unforeseen and not to be tolerated. The muster roll couldn't account for him other than as permitted to delay three months by Special Orders No. So-and-so, War Department, A.G.O., January 25, 1871. This gave Hodge unlooked-for reinforcements. A fortnight passed in March without a bid to dinner anywhere, without a request for further particulars as to Sir Galahad. So long as that interesting personage was expected any day to appear and answer for himself, it behooved Hodge to be measurably guarded in his statements, to keep within the limits of his authorities; but one day there came a letter from a lady at Department Head-Quarters to Mrs. Brooks, and before Brooks himself was made aware of the contents, he being at the club-room playing "pitch" and therefore beyond the pale of feminine consideration, the news was going the rounds of the garrison.

Mrs. Pelham, who was spending the winter in Washington, had written to an old and devoted friend of Major Waite's some very interesting news about Captain Barclay. The captain was in Washington a whole week, but had not called on Mrs. Pelham, though she had done everything

she could think of for him when he was wounded.
(The Pelhams were then at McPherson and near
old Waite's summer camp, but no one ever heard
of her ladyship's ever taking the faintest interest
in Barclay until after he developed into a mine-
owner and had been jilted by Laura Waite.) But
let Mrs. Pelham talk for herself, as she usually
did, as well as for every one else. "He spent the
first week in February here, leaving just before
poor Captain Lawrence came. No wonder he
didn't wish to meet him! And Mrs. Waite was
there, buttonholing everybody to get her pension
increased, and wearing the costliest crape you
ever saw, my dear, and—think of it!—solitaire
diamond ear-rings with it! She had a room in
a house where several prominent Congressmen
boarded, and was known as 'the fascinating
widow.' She sent to Barclay,—would you believe
it?—and begged him to come to see her, and he
actually did; and Mrs. Cutts, who lives in the
same house, told me that you ought to have seen
her that day,—no solitaire ear-rings or handsome
crape, mind you, but tears and bombazine; and
Mrs. Cutts vows that he gave her money. That
woman is angling for another husband, and has
been ever since poor Waite's death, and if anything were to happen to Mr. Winn it's just what
Laura would be doing too. It runs in the blood,

my dear. You know, and I know, that all the
time she was at Omaha Barracks and the major
in the field, she—a woman with a grown son and
a graduating daughter—was dancing with the
boys at the hops and riding—yes, and buggy-
riding—with bachelors like those wretches Gates
and Hagadorn." Buggy-riding was the unpar-
donable sin in Mrs. Pelham's eyes, she being "too
massive to sit in anything short of the side seat
of an ambulance," as said a regimental wit; and
Mrs. Pelham looked with eyes of disfavor on
women who managed to "keep their waists" as
Mrs. Waite did.

"But let me tell you about Captain Barclay,"
continued the letter. "General Corliss called to
see me two evenings ago and said he heard that
Barclay was actually a millionaire,—that he had
large interests in Nevada mines that were proving
fabulously rich. You can understand that I
wasn't at all surprised to hear that the general
had intimated to Mr. Ray, of his staff, that it
would be much better for him to go and serve
with his regiment awhile. Ray wouldn't be an
acceptable son-in-law; he has no money and too
many fascinations, and there are both the Corliss
girls, you know, to be provided for, and Miranda
is already *passé*, and Ray has resigned the place,
and the place is vacant, for—would you believe

it?—they say the general tendered it to Barclay, and Barclay declined. Why, when we were all at McPherson there wasn't anything satirical the Corlisses didn't say about Barclay, and now that he has money they bow down to and worship him." ("Something Mrs. Pelham wouldn't do for the world," said Mrs. Brooks to herself, with an odd smile.) "And when the general was asked about it yesterday he couldn't deny having made the offer, but said the reason Captain Barclay declined was that he would very probably resign in a few weeks, his business interests being such as to render it necessary for him to leave the army. So, my dear, you won't have the millionaire in Texas, after all, and I fancy how deeply Laura Winn will be disappointed. No matter how much she cares for her husband, she wouldn't be her mother's daughter if she didn't try to fascinate him over again."

Fancy the comfort of having such a letter as that to read to an appreciative audience! Mrs. Brooks fled with it to Mrs. Frazier, who thought it ought not to be read,—it was too like Dorothy Pelham for anything. But Mrs. Brooks took and read it to neighbors who were chatting and sewing together and had no such scruples. And that night it was dribbling about the post that Barclay had decided to resign, had refused a detail on the

staff of General Corliss: somebody else would get
Ned Lawrence's troop. Brooks heaved a sigh and
said to himself he was glad of it, and the women
heaved a sigh and wished he might have come, if
only for a little while, just to make things interesting: "it would be such a novelty to have a
millionaire mine-owner in garrison and actually
doing duty as a captain of cavalry." Finally they
began to wonder what Mrs. Winn would say now,
she having had nothing at all to say.

That very evening it chanced to occur to Mr.
Hodge that he had not returned Lieutenant
Winn's call (by card,—the cavalryman having
dropped in when he knew the new arrival to have
dropped out), and when Hodge presented himself
at the Winns' (he had spoken of his intention at
mess in the presence and hearing of the negro attendant, who had mentioned it without delay to
the Winns' colored combination of cook and
serving-maid, who had come over to borrow a cup
of cooking sherry, it being too far to the sutler's,
and that damsel had duly notified her mistress of
the intended honor), he was shown into the dimly
lighted army sitting-room, where, toasting her
feet before the fire, sat dreaming the young mistress of the establishment, who started up in apparent surprise. She had heard neither the step
nor the ring. Very possibly she was dozing, she

admitted, for baby was sleeping aloft and her husband was gone. She was attired in a silken gown that Hodge described somewhat later at the major's as "puffickly stunning,"—a garment that revealed the rich curves of her beautiful throat and neck and arms; women who heard wondered why she should be wearing that most becoming evening robe when there was not even a hop. She looked handsomer than the gown, said Hodge, as she rose and greeted him, her cheeks flushed, her eyes languorous and smouldering at first, then growing slowly brilliant. She apologized for the absence of Mr. Winn. He was spending much time at the office just now. "He is regimental commissary, you know, or at least he has been," she explained. Hodge knew all about that, and he also knew that if what he heard about the post was true it would have been better had Winn spent more time at the office before. Then Mrs. Winn was moved to be gracious. She had heard so many, many pleasant things of Mr. Hodge since his arrival. She was so honored that he should call when he must be having so many claims on his time, so many dinner-calls to pay. She and Mr. Winn were so sorry they had been unable to entertain Mr. Hodge, but, until the cook they were expecting from San Antonio came, they were positively starving, and could invite no

one to share their scraps. "That cook has been
expected a whole year," said other women, but
Mrs. Winn paraded him as the cause of her social
short-comings as confidently as ever. Then Mrs.
Winn went on to speak of how much she had
heard of Hodge at Omaha,—dear Omaha.
"What lovely times we had along the Platte in
the good old days!" Hodge blushed with joy,
and preened and twittered and thought how
blessed a thing it was to be welcomed to the fire-
side of such a belle and beauty and to be remembered by her as one of the gay young bachelors at
Sidney. "Such wicked stories as we heard of you
scapegraces from time to time," said she, whereat
Hodge looked as though he might, indeed, have
been shockingly wicked, as perhaps he had. Indeed, she feared they, the young officers, were "a
sad lot, a sad lot," and looked up at him from
under the drooping lashes in a way that prompted
him to an inspiration that was almost electric in
its effect on him. Hodge fairly seemed to sparkle,
to scintillate. "Sad! We were in despair," said
he, "but that was when we heard of your engagement—oh, ah, the second one, I mean," he stumbled on, for it would never do, thought he, to
mention the first.

But he need have had no hesitation. Laura
Winn had heard from other and obscurer sources

something of the rumors floating over the post that very day. She had planned to drop in at the colonel's, where the Fraziers entertained at dinner and music that very evening, in hopes of hearing accidentally something definite, for Winn was one of those useless husbands who never hear anything of current gossip. But women might not talk if they thought she wished to hear, and fate had provided her a better means. She saw here and now the opportunity and the man. It was Hodge who had told so much that was of vivid interest to her. It was Hodge she had been longing to meet for days, but Winn had held him aloof, and now here she had this ingenuous repository of Barclayisms all to herself until Winn should return; the chance was not to be lost.

"I love to live over those dear old days when I was a girl," she said. "Friends seemed so real then, men so true, life so buoyant. Sometimes I find myself wishing there were more of the old friends, the old set, here. We seem—so much more to each other, don't you know, Mr. Hodge?" And Hodge felt sure "we" did, and hitched his chair a foot nearer the fire.

"Of course I was younger then, and knew so little of the world, and yet, knowing it as I do now—I can say this to you, you know, Mr. Hodge,—I couldn't to another soul here, for you were *of* us, you served with father's column" (Hodge's service was limited .to playing poker with "those wretches Gates and Hagadorn" and others of Waite's command on one or two memorable occasions, and the resultant hole in his purse was neither as broad as a church nor deep as a well, but 'twould serve). "I've often felt here as though I would give anything to see some of the dear old crowd; not that people are not very lovely here, but, you know, we army friends cling so to the old associations." And now the beautiful eyes seemed almost suffused, and Hodge waxed eloquent.

"I am thrice fortunate," said he, recalling the lines of his Maltravers, "in that I am numbered among them." And now, like Laura, he looked upon Worth as cold and dormant as compared with the kindling friendships of the distant Platte.

"Indeed you are!" said she. "You bring back the sweetest days of my life, and some of the saddest. I have no one to speak to me, you know, —of course—until you did a moment ago. Tell me, is—is his life so changed as—as they say it is?"

"I never saw a man so broke up," he responded. "He never smiled after you—after—after it was broken off, you know." Barclay's smile was as rare as a straight flush anyhow, he admitted to himself, but the assertion sounded well.

"And—of late—what have you heard of him?" she asked. And Hodge poured forth his latest news, and added more. He, too, he said, had had a letter from an intimate friend. Captain Barclay had declared that the assignment to the Twelfth Cavalry was impossible, Texas was impossible. His business interests would necessitate his declining if, indeed, there were no other reasons. General Corliss had tendered him the position of aide-de-camp and made Billy Ray of the —th resign to make way for him, and the moment Barclay found that out he went to Ray and told him the whole business was without his (Barclay's) knowledge, and sooner than displace him he would refuse. "Yes," said Hodge, "that's the way my friend heard it from Ray himself. Now, if Barclay could only get a detail on McDowell's staff in California it would have suited him to a tee; then he could have looked after his Nevada interests and his Wyoming pensioners too."

Did Mr. Hodge know surely about Mr. Barclay's wealth? Was it all true? he was asked.

Oh, yes, there wasn't a doubt of it, said Hodge. It was just another of those cases where a man had money in abundance, and yet would have given it all, he added, sentimentally, but here she uplifted rebukingly her white, slim hand,—or was it warningly? for there came a quick footfall on the porch without. The hall door opened sharply, letting in a gust of cold night wind, and, throwing off his cavalry cape with its faded yellow lining, Lieutenant Winn strode through the hallway into his little den at the rear.

"You will come and see me again," she murmured low, while yet the footsteps resounded, "it has been so—good to see you,—so like old times. We'll have to talk of other things now. Mr. Winn doesn't like old times too well."

But Mr. Winn never so much as looked in the parlor door until she called to him. Then, as she saw his face, the young wife arose with anxiety in her own.

"What is it? Where are you going—with your revolver, too? Mr. Hodge, dear."

"Oh-h! Beg pardon, Mr. Hodge. Glad to see you," was Winn's distraught acknowledgment of the presence of the visitor, as he extended a reluctant hand. "My sergeant can't be found," he went on, hurriedly. "They say he's gone to Fuller's ranch, and it may be all right, but the colonel has ordered out a patrol to fetch him back. Don't worry, Laurie; I may have to ride out with it."

And hurriedly he kissed her and bounded down the steps.

For a moment she stood in the doorway, the light from the hall lamp shining on her dusky hair and proud, beautiful face, forgetful of the man who stood gazing at her. Then with a shiver she suddenly turned.

"It's the second time that Sergeant Marsden has been missed in just this way, when he was most needed, and—it's so imprudent, so—and my husband is so imprudent, so unsuspicious. Mr. Hodge," she cried, impulsively, "if you've heard anything, or if you do hear anything, about him or Mr. Winn, be a friend to me and tell me, won't you?" And there was nothing Hodge would not have promised, nothing he would not have told, but the door of the adjoining quarters slammed, an officer came striding along the porch common to the double set, and the clank of a sabre was heard as he neared them.

"Winn gone?" he asked. "Don't worry, Mrs. Winn. We'll overhaul that scoundrel before he can reach the settlements, unless——"

"But what is wrong? What has happened, Mr. Brayton?" she asked, her face white with dread, her heart fluttering.

"My Lord, Mrs. Winn, I beg your pardon! I supposed of course he had told you. Marsden's bolted. Colonel Riggs, the inspector-general, got here to-night with Captain Barclay, instead of coming by regular stage Saturday, and Marsden lit out the moment he heard of their arrival. Of course we hope Winn isn't badly bitten."

But her thoughts were of another matter now. "Captain Barclay," she faltered, "here? Why, I—I heard——"

"Yes," shouted the young officer, as he went clattering down the steps. "'Scuse me—I've got to mount at once," as an orderly came running up at the moment with his horse. "Riggs has come, post-haste, only Barclay and one man with him besides the driver. It's lucky that Friday gang never got wind of it."

CHAPTER IV.

For forty-eight hours Fort Worth was in turmoil. To begin with, the sudden, unheralded advent of a department inspector in those days meant something ominous, and from Frazier down to the drum-boys the garrison scented mischief the moment that familiar old black-hooded, dust-covered spring wagon, drawn by the famous six-mule team, came spinning in across the *mesa* just after retreat, no escort whatever being in sight. Cavalrymen had trotted alongside, said Riggs, from two of the camps on the way, but they had made that long day's drive from Crockett Springs all alone, trusting to luck that the Friday gang, so called, would not get wind of it. Just who and how many constituted that array of outlaws no man, including its own membership, could accurately say. Two paymasters, two wagon-trains, and no end of mail-stages had been "jumped" by those enterprising road agents in the course of the five years that followed the war, and not once had a conviction occurred. Arrests had been made by marshals, sheriffs, and officers in command of detachments, but a more innocent lot of victims, according to the testi-

mony of friends and fellow-citizens, never dwelt
in Dixie. Three only of their number had been
killed and left for recognition in the course of
those three years. One only of these was known,
and the so-called Friday gang managed to sur-
round its haunts, its movements, and its membership with a mystery that defied civil officials and
baffled the military. Escorts the size of a cavalry
platoon had been needed every time a disbursing
officer went to and fro, and a sizable squad accompanied the stage whenever it carried even a
moderate amount of treasure. At three points
along the road from the old Mexican capital to
the outlying posts, strong detachments of cavalry
had been placed in camp, so that relays of escorts
might be on hand when needed. At three different times within the past two years, strong
posses had gone with the civil officials far into the
foot-hills in search of the haunts of the band, but
no occupied haunt was ever found, no band of any
size or consequence ever encountered; yet depredations were incessant. The mail-stage came and
went with guarded deliberation. The quartermaster's trains were accompanied by at least a
company of infantry. The sutler's wagons
travelled with the quartermaster's train, and the
sutler's money went to San Antonio only when
the quartermaster and commissary sent theirs,

and then a whole squadron had been known to ride in charge. Anything from a wagon-train down to a buckboard was game for the gang, and soldiers, ranchmen, and prospectors told stories of having been halted, overhauled, and searched by its masked members at various times, and, whether found plethoric or poor, having been hospitably entertained as soon as robbed of all they possessed. Only four days before Riggs made his venturesome dash, three discharged soldiers, filled with impatience and whiskey, had sought to run the gauntlet to the camp at Crockett's, and came back, in the robbers' cast-off clothing, to "take on" for another term, having parted with their uniforms and the savings of several years at the solicitation of courteous strangers they met along the route. Nothing but an emergency could have brought Riggs, full tilt, for he was getting along in years and loved the comforts of his army home.

Emergency it was, as he explained to Frazier instantly on his arrival. The general had indubitable information that ranches to the south had long been buying government stores, bacon, feed, flour, coffee, etc. The source of their supply could only be the warehouses at Worth, and Marsden was a "swell" sergeant, whose airs and affluence had made him the object of suspicion. Those were the days when cavalry regiments had

a commissary, but Congress did away with the
office, and Winn, whom an indulgent colonel had
detailed to that supposedly "soft snap" when
regimental head-quarters were stationed at Worth,
had been left there with his bulky array of
boxes and barrels when the colonel and staff
were transferred to a more southern post, the un-
derstanding being that he was to turn over everything to Frazier's new quartermaster as soon as
that official should arrive. Frazier's appointee,
however, was a lieutenant from a distant station.
The War Department had not improved the ap-
pointment when made. Correspondence had been
going on, and only within the week was notification received that the choice was finally confirmed
and that Lieutenant Trott would soon arrive.
Meantime Winn remained, but the stores were
going. Somebody had money enough to bribe
the sentries nightly posted at the storehouse at
the northern corner of the big rectangle, and
wagon-load after wagon-load must have been
driven away. Outwardly, as developed by the
count made early on the morning following
Riggs's coming, all was right, but a veteran
cavalry sergeant scoffingly knocked in the heads
of cask, box, and barrel, and showed how bacon
by the cord had been replaced by rags and boulders, sugar, coffee, and flour by bushels of sand,

molasses and vinegar by branch water, and tea
and tobacco by trash. "Two to three thousand
dollars' worth of rations gone," said Riggs, at
noon, "and the devil to pay if Winn cannot."
Vain the night ride to Fuller's ranch in search of
Marsden. That worthy had long since feathered
his portable nest, and on one of the quartermaster's best horses had left the post within the half-
hour of Riggs's coming, no man knew for what
point after once he crossed the ford. Hoof-tracks
by the hundred criss-crossed and zigzagged over
the southward *mesa.* Thick darkness had settled
down. Fuller's people swore no signs of him
had been seen, and, though patrols kept on all
night, poor Winn came back despairing an hour
before the dawn to face his fate; even at noon he
had hardly begun to realize the extent of his over-
whelming loss.

"Go home and try to sleep," said the colonel,
sadly, to the dumb and stricken man. "You can
do no good here. I'll send the doctor to you."

But Winn started up and shook the old fellow's
kindly hand. "I cannot go. My God! I must
know the whole business," he cried. "I cannot
sleep or eat a morsel."

"Whatever you do, don't drink," said Riggs,
in not unkindly warning. "Go and see your wife,
anyhow, for an hour or so. She has sent three

times." But words were useless. Sympathetic
comrades came and strove with him and said
empty words of hope or cheer,—empty, because
they knew poor Winn had not a soul in the world
to whom to look for help. Kin to half a dozen
old army names, it helped him not a whit, for no
one of them was blessed with means beyond the
monthly pay, and some had not even that un-
mortgaged. Twenty-five hundred dollars' shortage already, to say nothing of the cash for recent
sales, and more, no doubt, to come. The very
thought was ruin. Refusing comfort, the hapless
man sat down at his littered desk, stared again at
the crowded, dusty pigeon-holes, and saw nothing,
nothing but misery, if not despair.

Brayton went over at luncheon-time and
begged a word with Mrs. Winn. She peered
over the balustrade from the second story, with
big, black-rimmed eyes, but could not come down,
could not leave baby, who was fretful, she said.
Oh, why didn't Mr. Winn come home? What
good did it do to stay over there and worry?
When would they get through? Brayton couldn't
say, but Winn couldn't come,—felt he must stay
at the office; but if Mrs. Winn would have some
tea and a bite of luncheon prepared, he, Brayton,
would gladly take it over. Yet even this friendly
office seemed to bring no solace. Winn barely

sipped the tea or tasted the savory broth. Frazier
and Riggs went out to luncheon, leaving him still
seated at his desk; and their faces were black
with gloom when they reached the colonel's door.
Winn's distressing plight, following so shortly
after the dire misfortune that had happened to
Lawrence, would have saddened the whole garrison and tinged all table-talk with melancholy
but for the blessed antidote afforded in Captain
Barclay's sudden and most unlooked-for coming.

And what a surprise it was! All one afternoon
and part of one evening had Fort Worth been telling that Captain Barclay had refused the assignment to a regiment and post where he must meet
Laura Winn; that he had resigned rather than
encounter once more the woman who had played
him false; that he was too wealthy to care to bury
himself in this out-of-the-way hole in Texas anyhow; and even while they were talking, all unheralded, here he was. The major's hospitable
doors opened to receive him within ten minutes
of his dust-covered advent, and only by hearsay
all that night could the garrison know of his presence. One small sole-leather trunk, with the
travelling-bag, rifle, field-glasses, canteen, and
lunch-box, constituted all the personal luggage
of the new arrival. It could not even be said
that any one outside of Brooks's had even seen

him, so coated with dust were the contents of that
old spring wagon when unloaded at the colonel's
steps; and many a woman hastened to her door
on the following morning, attracted thither by
the announcement that Captain Barclay was on
the major's porch.

There, with his host, he stood for quite a while,
the major pointing out the landmarks along the
westward range, and indicating, apparently, other
features in the landscape.   One or two officers,
hastening by, raised their caps or ran up the
steps and shook hands with the new-comer, but
he was presently summoned in to breakfast, and
neighbors could only say he was not very tall, not
very stout, not very slight, not very anything.
Captain De Lancy, who had had three minutes'
conversation, said he "seemed pleasant," but that
was all.   Mrs. De Lancy was confirmed in her
preconceived opinion that men were owls, because her husband was unable to add to the military descriptive list of brown eyes, brown hair,
brown beard and clothes, any of the particulars
she sought.   He couldn't tell whether Barclay
had fine teeth or good complexion, what his
mouth was like, whether he had nice hands and
voice.   Indeed, he couldn't see why Mrs. De
Lancy should be so anxious to know.   Not until
towards noon was any reliable particular concern-

ing Captain Barclay passed along the line. Then
the domestic bulletin dealt out the fact that the
millionaire mine-owner wore a flannel shirt and
a silver watch, which information was distinctly
disheartening.

But that evening, while the colonel and other
officers began calling at Brooks's to welcome formally the unexpected addition to the commissioned force, Mrs. Brooks was able to slip out and
over to her crony, Mrs. De Lancy, and in ten
minutes she had an audience, married and single,
that gladdened her heart. She could and did talk
almost uninterruptedly for over an hour. Ar-
riving dames or damsels were signalled not to in-
terrupt, and, joining the circle, patiently with-
held their questions until she paused for breath;
and then what every one seemed to want to know
was, had he said anything or asked anything about
Mrs. Winn? He had. He expressed the utmost
sympathy with poor Mr. Winn. He told Major
Brooks of a similar experience that occurred in
the —d Cavalry only the year previous, and how
it would probably take the defrauded officer years
to square the account. He most delicately inquired as to the general health and well-being of
Mrs. Winn, whom he had had the pleasure, he
said, of meeting several years before; but more
particularly he had asked about Lawrence, and

Lawrence's children, and who was in charge of
them; it was evident that he was deeply concerned about them and most anxious to meet Captain and Mrs. Blythe.

"Well, that's one thing at least in his favor,"
was the verdict; for throughout Brooks's **battalion**, as it was then called, or squadron, as we
should call it to-day, there existed an indefinable
feeling of antagonism towards this stranger within
their gates, thus coming to usurp the place Ned
Lawrence held in their hearts and homes, if no
longer on their rolls. Some one slipped out and
brought in Mrs. Blythe, for whose benefit Mrs.
Brooks not unwillingly went over all she had told
about Captain Barclay's queries as to the children
and their benefactors; and that sweet, tender-
hearted, motherly woman ought to have softened
to him, but didn't. "He could have heard it all
at San Antonio for the asking," she declared.
"But he didn't stop two days at San Antonio,"
explained Mrs. Brooks. "The moment he heard
that Colonel Riggs was going on by special ambulance he begged to be allowed to go with him,
and Riggs couldn't see a way to say no, and later
confessed he was very glad he had said yes."

"Brooks, you were all growling at the idea of
having any outsider, much less a doughboy, take
Lawrence's place," were the bluff old veteran's

exact words; "but you mark what I say. I was
rather prejudiced against this young fellow myself, and it has just taken this jolt together from
San Antonio to satisfy me he is grit to the back-
bone, and you are in big luck to get him."

At least a dozen men called at the major's that
evening to pay their respects to the new comrade.
It was long after taps when the last one left, but,
almost to a man, they gathered at the club-room
later to compare notes. Hodge, of course, had
called among the first, his claim of intimate or at
least old acquaintance rendering it necessary.
Barclay's brown eyes certainly lighted at the sight
of the face he had known in the far northwest;
he chatted for a moment with the infantryman,
and expressed his pleasure at meeting him again.
Then Blythe entered, with his grave, massive face
and courteous yet reserved manner; and Brooks
spoke of the fact that Barclay seemed to shake
hands more earnestly with him than with any of
the others, and to look at him oftener, though
striving to slight no one. They sat there, as men
will at such times, somewhat awkwardly, only one
speaking at once, and generally the same one.
Hodge, for instance, had much to say and many
questions to ask about fellows he had known in
Wyoming, and when he left and others came in,
three or four went at the same time, having sat

stolid listeners, calmly studying Barclay with their eyes and finally saying good-night, and "hope to see you when you get settled," etc.

They were talking of him at the store, and wondering when and where he would settle, and whether he would take Lawrence's quarters, and what would then become of Ada and little Jim, who with old Mammy still occupied their rooms there and had all the furniture as poor daddy left it, but who went over to the Blythes' three times a day to take their rations with their army chums and playmates, the little Blythes. "What a god-send it would be if he would buy poor Ned's books and furniture!" said De Lancy. "It would yield enough to send those poor babies home."

"Home," said Blythe, sadly: "what home has a child whose kith and kin are all of the army? They have neither home nor mother."

But no man made the faintest comment on facts the women remarked instanter, that Barclay's watch was only silver and his guard an inexpensive little cord or braid of fine leather, worn about his neck; that his travelling suit was of rough gray mixture, and his shirt a flannel *négligé.* But then, as Mrs. De Lancy explained in extenuation of their blindness, he had donned his uniform by the time they called that second evening, and it became him very well.

CHAPTER V.

A WEEK went rapidly by. Captain Barclay had gone on duty, and Mr. Brayton, his sub, had not yet "sized him up." Lieutenant Trott, the new regimental quartermaster, had arrived by the Saturday's stage, and was ready to receipt to Lieutenant Winn for all property he had to turn over; but Winn had broken down under his weight of woe and taken to his bed. From Washington came tidings, telegraphed as far as San Antonio, that Lawrence was slowly mending and would soon be sitting up. Mrs. Winn, absorbed in the care of her suffering husband, had accepted no invitations, but the many sympathetic women who called to ask if there were not some way in which they could be of aid reported her as looking feverish and far from well. Some of them had ventured to speak of the new arrival, and, though her ears were evidently open, her lips were closed. That she was willing, if not eager, to hear anything they had to say or tell about Captain Barclay was all very well as far as it went, but what some of her visitors most desired was to hear what she had to say about him; as she would say nothing, one or two had resorted to a little delicate questioning in the hope of drawing her out. Mrs. Faulkner, a young matron of her own age and previous social standing, an army girl like herself, and for some time her one intimate friend at Worth, went so far as to ask, "You used to know him very well, did you not?" and was checkmated by the answer, "Not well enough to talk about," which answer Mrs. Faulkner pondered over and considered deliberately and inexcusably rude. With the kindest feeling for her in the world, as all the women avowed, and no animosity whatever towards Barclay over and beyond that feeling on poor Colonel Lawrence's account, there was the liveliest interest at Worth as regarded Mrs. Winn and Captain Barclay in seeing what they would do; and, to the disappointment of all Fort Worth, they had done nothing.

Barclay promptly returned the calls of the officers who had called upon him, and had done all proper homage to the wives of those who were possessed of such blessings, but there were still certain quarters where his face or his card had not been seen: at Captain Cram's, for instance, because that warrior was on scout and couldn't call, ditto his lieutenant; at one or two of the new and unpolished pillars of the temple, because they had not known enough or had been too shy to call; and at Winn's, because that officer was ill of a fever and could not call. There was another set of quarters in which he had not yet set foot, —Ned Lawrence's; and that was the house most people expected him to visit first.

Nor did he remain at Brooks's. The major's house was big, but so was his household. "You have a vacant room here, Mr. Brayton," he said, the third day after his arrival, as he dropped in at his subaltern's. "It may be a month before I get shaken down into place. I dislike to disturb women and children, and so have decided to ask you to let me move my cot and trunk in here awhile and to propose my name at the mess." And Brayton, blushing at the realization of the fact that the furniture in the room referred to consisted solely of some chairs, a square pine table covered with a cavalry blanket, with a cigar-box half full of smoking-tobacco, another half full of white beans, and a pack of cards for its sole ornaments, nevertheless bravely ushered his new captain into the bower, and Barclay looked neither surprised nor satirical at the sight. "We sometimes play a mild game of draw here, sir," said downright Brayton, "which accounts for the appearance of things; but my striker can clean it up in ten minutes, and you are most welcome."

"It won't put you out in any way?" asked Barclay, without the comment of an uplifted eyebrow on the evidence adduced.

"Not so much as poker, if it does at all," said Brayton, promptly. He was determined his captain should know the extent of his frailties at the start.

Barclay smiled quietly and turned to the boy with liking in his eye. "I'm hardly ten years your senior, Brayton," said he, "and so shall not preach, but I believe we can put that room to a little better use."

The next day he took his seat at the bachelors' mess, where a dozen officers were congregated, all of them but two his juniors in rank. The sideboard was lavishly decked with the indispensables of that benighted day. The old-timers and the new took their anteprandial cocktail or toddy, and hospitably invited Barclay to join. Barclay smiled gratefully, but said he had "never yet got in the way of it, somehow," nor did he more than sip at the Bordeaux which the presiding officer ordered served in honor of the occasion. The mess was rather silent. Most men seemed desirous of listening to Barclay when he spoke at all. They knew every twist and turn of each other's mode of speech by that time, and could repeat verbatim every story in the combination.

Barclay might have something new; but if he did he had no chance. Captain Follansbee took and kept the floor from first to last. He was airing his views on the subject of consolidation, reorganization, and purification as practised at the War Department, a topic which the others considered inexcusable, not so much from the fact that it must be most unpalatable to Captain Barclay, a beneficiary of the business, as it turned out, as because Follansbee had worn them all out with it weeks before.

And, to everybody's surprise, so far from seeming annoyed or embarrassed or bored, Barclay led him on from point to point, and, even after coffee was served, sat an apparently absorbed listener, for by that time Follansbee had absorbed most of the claret and was dilating on the matter with especial reference to the case of Colonel Lawrence. Later that evening Barclay spent an hour at the Blythes', and two days after he and Brayton dined there.

It was a seven-o'clock dinner. The doctor and his wife, Major and Mrs. Brooks, Miss Frazier and Miss Amanda Frazier, were the other guests. Those were the days when officers of all grades wore epaulets when in full uniform, but, except in one or two swell messes, full dress was not considered requisite for either dinner or hops. The

men wore the uniform frock-coat with shoulder-
straps; some few privileged characters even
dared to appear in a sack-coat with white tie.
Such a thing as the evening dress of civil life was
unknown at a military post, and unowned in the
fighting force of the army, outside, perhaps, of
the artillery. The doctor was a privileged character, a man who said what he thought and did
what he thought right; and when Mrs. Blythe,
glancing out of her parlor window, saw their
favored friend and medical adviser coming along
the walk, his hands deep in his trousers-pockets
and himself in a fit of abstraction and a new sack-
coat, while the partner of his joys and sorrows
chatted briskly with the Frazier girls, Mrs. Blythe
called up-stairs to her massive liege lord, "Wear
your blouse, dear; the doctor has on his"; whereupon Blythe slipped out of the uniform coat of
formal cut and into the easy sack, and came trotting down the creaking stair in time to welcome
his guests. Brooks, Barclay, and Brayton, who
came later, were in the prescribed regulation
dress, whereat Dr. Collabone exclaimed, "Hullo!
Now that's what I ought to have done, if I'd had
as much regard for conventionality as I have for
health. Gentlemen, do you know you simply
invite an apoplectic seizure by sitting down to
dinner in a tightly buttoned uniform coat? It

is barbarous. There ought to be a regulation against it."

It was observed that while the doctor included all three of the cavalrymen in his remarks he looked at and apparently addressed only one, Captain Barclay, whose uniform coat was brand-new, very handsomely cut, its buttons and shoulder-straps of the finest make and finish, whereas the doctor's were tarnished, if not actually shabby. Brooks frowned, and Brayton looked embarrassed lest Barclay should take it amiss; but that officer remained smilingly interested, and in nowise troubled. The Frazier girls giggled, and Miss Amanda was prompt to assert that for her part she loved to see the officers wear the proper uniform, and she wasn't alarmed about apoplexy; whereupon Collabone smiled benignly and said, "What did I tell you about the danger of tight lacing?" Amanda couldn't bear the doctor. Her elder and primmer sister only half liked him. Many of the women thought him brusque and rude, but officers and men and mothers of families swore by him, and children adored him. A child-less man himself, he seemed to keep open house for the offspring of his comrades. They swarmed about his quarters at all hours of the day. They invaded his parlor, overflowed his dining-room, and ruled his kitchen.

A kindly and placid soul was Mrs. Collabone, a woman who had few cares or perplexities, and these she promptly turned over to her broad-minded, broad-shouldered liege for final disposition, as serenely confident of their speedy dissipation as she was of the prompt conquest of any and all the manifold ills to which childish flesh is heir by that practitioner's infallible remedies. Children ran loose in those days in Texas; and so they ought to, said Collabone. "Savage races are the only scientific rearers," he maintained. "Boys or girls, they should be burdened with but a single garment, or less, from the time they're born until they're eight or ten, and meantime they should be made to eat, sleep, and live out-doors." He preached for children regularity in matters of diet, prescribed four light meals a day, practised heterodoxy, and distributed bread and milk, bread and syrup, bread and jam, cookies, corn dodgers, and molasses candy, morning, noon, and night. Aunt Purlina, the fat and jocund goddess of the Collabones' kitchen, had standing orders on such subjects, and many a time had the post surgeon to wait for his own refreshments because "the kids" had possession of the premises. There was never a worry along officers' row when children strayed from home. "Oh, they're over at the doctor's," was the soothing response to all

queries. The doctor's big yard was the garrison
play-ground; for, when a soulless, heartless, child-
less, wifeless post commander, Frazier's predecessor, had dared to prohibit the use of the parade-
ground for croquet, hop-scotch, marbles, or "Tom,
Tom Pull-away," it was Collabone who rigged up
swings and giant strides at his own expense and
without the aid of the post quartermaster, and
sent away to New Orleans for croquet sets for the
exclusive use of the youngsters. It nettled in-
expressibly the field officer commanding. He
took it as a rebuke from his junior, and took it
out in a course of nagging and persecution at the
doctor's expense, that roused the energies of the
entire post. Frazier was sent from Concho to
supersede the objectionable lieutenant-colonel,
who thereupon declared his intention of moving
the doctor out and taking his quarters; but a
courier galloped all the way from Worth to the
camp at San Patricio, whither the department
commander had gone a-hunting, and another got
back in the nick of time with orders for the de-
vastating officer to move to the cantonment on
the Pecos, the worst hole in all Texas, as reported
by the department inspector. The children had
won the day.

At the very moment when the party took their
seats at Blythe's, the children of that establish-

ment and their friends the Lawrences were holding high carnival at the doctor's, Aunt Purlina
and the colored maid vying with each other in
efforts to stuff them to repletion. Over this up-
roarious feast presided the tall slip of a damsel
with whom poor Ned had parted so mournfully
when he went away in February. Ada's was the
only face in all the merry party that seemed to
have known a trace of sorrow. Her big, dark,
mournful eyes and shaggy hair, her sallow face
and shabby frock, twice let down and still
"skimpy," told a pathetic story. Thirteen years
of age, the child had already seen much of anxiety
and trouble,—much, indeed, beyond the ken of
many an elder; and the week going by brought
hour after hour of nervous wear and tear, the
cause of which only one woman knew, and strove
in vain to banish. Ada shrank with actual dread
and repulsion from the thought of having to meet
the man who had come to take her loved father's
place.

Thrice had Barclay spoken to Mrs. Blythe of a
desire to see the children of Colonel Lawrence;
now he felt confident that he knew the cause of
her evasion, and pressed no more. But all through
dinner, even while speaking in the low, somewhat
measured tones habitual to him, he lost no talk
in which the children were mentioned; and at

Blythe's they were never forgotten. It was not long before he discovered that the Blythes and Lawrences—the young people—were at the doctor's, Ada presiding. Indeed, with much gusto, almost as soon as soup was served, Collabone began telling of her matronly, motherly ways. Half an hour later a messenger came to the door and asked if Dr. Collabone would please step over and see Mrs. De Lancy a moment. "Tell her I'll be there in just one hour," said the doctor, looking at his watch. Then he added, for the benefit of the party present, "There's nothing in the world the matter with Mrs. De Lancy, and by that time she'll have forgotten she sent for me." Ten minutes later came another call. It was the Collabones' domestic this time. "Little Jimmy's cut his hand, and Miss Ada can't stop the bleeding." "Say I'll come instantly," said he, springing from the table and making his excuses to the lady of the house.

Barclay's face shone with instant sympathy and interest. Dessert was nearly over. He turned to the motherly woman whose own gentle face betrayed her anxiety.

"Will you think me very rude?" he said. "You know I do not smoke, and I do want so much to meet those children. I feel that Ada purposely shuns me, and this is an opportunity not to be lost. May I be excused? I will soon return." Mrs. Blythe's eyes were eloquent as she bade him go.

Three minutes later he softly entered the doctor's sitting-room. There in a big easy-chair sat a tall, sallow-faced, tumbled-haired girl, holding in her arms a burly little fellow whose frightened sobbings she had at last controlled, and who, with only an occasional whimper, was now submitting to the doctor's examination and deriving much comfort from his professional and reassuring manner.

"Why, this is no cut at all, Jimmy, my boy. The reason you bled so much is that you are so uncommonly healthy and full of blood. This won't keep you out of mischief six hours. Hold the basin steady, Purlina. Kick all you want to, Jimmy. Don't you dare to laugh, Kittie Blythe. Well, if here isn't Captain Barclay, too, come in to see you! Here is the little wounded soldier, captain. You had your arm in a sling six long months, didn't you? The Sioux did that for him, Jimmy, and you've only got to be done up in a bandage till to-morrow night. Let Captain Barclay hold you? Indeed I won't. He doesn't know how to hold little boys—like Ada. He's got no little boys, nor big Ada either. Bet your boots he wishes he had, Jimmy." Thus the doc-

tor chatted as he bathed and bandaged the pudgy
little fist, while Jimmy lay, half relieved at the
rapid termination to his woes, half resentful they
should be declared so trifling, and, with eyes
much swollen with weeping, critically studied the
new captain's appearance and gave token of modi-
fied approval. But Ada's white lids and long
dark lashes were never once uplifted.

Presently Collabone pronounced everything
doing finely, and said he'd go and see Mrs. De
Lancy. "You tell them there's nothing much the
matter, will you?" he said to Barclay.

"I will—when I get there," was the smiling
reply; "but I'm going to tell this little fellow a
story first about a Sioux baby boy I knew in Wyoming, and his playmate, a baby bear." And,
with wondering, wide-open eyes upon him, Barclay seated himself close to Ada's chair, while the
doctor stole silently away.

Half an hour later, when he returned, a circle
of absorbed listeners was gazing into Barclay's
face. Ada only sat apart, and little Jimmy's
curly head was pillowed on the story-teller's
breast.

CHAPTER VI.

TEN days passed. Barclay had become an institution at Fort Worth, yet opinions were as divided and talk of him as constant as before he came. First and foremost, he had met Mrs. Winn, and his demeanor on that presumably trying occasion had proved a distinct disappointment. Winn was recovering health, if not spirits. A stage-load of officers and ladies had come from the cantonment to spend forty-eight hours, and a big dance was prescribed for their benefit. Mrs. Winn danced divinely, and never looked so well as when with a suitable partner on a suitable floor. Those were the days when we raved over the "Mabel," the "Guards," the "Maude," and the "Hilda" waltzes, Godfrey's melodious creations,—when the galop and *trois temps* were going out, and we "Boston dipped" to every tune from Pat Malloy to Five O'Clock in the Morning, and the Worth orchestra was a good one when the first violin wasn't drunk, a condition which had to be provided against with assiduous care. The party arrived during one of his lucid

76

intervals, and the adjutant promptly placed the
artist under bonds to shun the cup until after the
guests had gone; then he could fill up to his
heart's content and no fear of a fine. Winn
couldn't attend, but Laura was looking wan and
sallow. She needed air and exercise, and her husband urged her to accept Mr. Brayton's escort
and go; so did Collabone; so did her own inclination. Superbly gowned and coiffed and otherwise
decorated, she went, and her entrance was the
sensation of the evening. It was long after ten
when she appeared. The hop was in full blast;
the big room, gayly decorated, was throbbing
with the rhythmic movement of the closing figure
of the Lancers. Almost everybody was on the
floor, for energetic were our dancers in those bygone days. Just as the music came to full stop,
and with joyous laughter and merry words of
parting the sets broke up, the women and girls,
middle-aged or young (they never grow old in the
army), clinging to their partners' arms, fanning,
possibly, their flushed faces, were escorted to their
seats, and the floor like magic was cleared for the
coming waltz. The group at the flag-draped entrance parted right and left, making way for a
young officer in cavalry uniform at whom nobody
so much as glanced, because of the tall and radiant woman at his side, on whom all eyes were

centred. "Look at Laura Winn," was the whisper that flew from womanly lip to lip. "Isn't she
simply superb?" "Look at Mrs. Winn," muttered many a man, his eyes lighting at the sight.
"Isn't she just stunning?"

And then people began to hunt for Barclay.

He was standing at the moment talking quietly
with Mrs. Frazier, who was making much of
the young captain now, and was accused of
having hopes of him on account of her eldest
darling, who had dined by his side three different
times at three different houses during the week,
and was therefore said to be "receiving considerable attention." But the hush of laughter and
miscellaneous chatter almost instantly attracted
the matron's attention. She glanced at the door,
gasped involuntarily, and then as suddenly turned
and narrowly watched him, for he too noted the
lull in conversation, and, slowly facing the doorway, saw before him not ten paces away the
woman who was to have been his wife, gazing
straight at him as though challenging him to look
and be blinded, as blinded by her beauty he had
been before. She was only a young, immature,
untaught girl then, ignorant of her powers. Now
the soft bloom was gone, but in its place there
lurked among the tiny threads of lines or wrinkles
just forming at the corners of her brilliant eyes,

and in the witching curves about her mobile, sensitive, exquisite lips, a charm beside which her virgin graces were cold and formal. She had been what all men called a wonderfully pretty girl. She was now what many women termed a dangerously beautiful woman, and she knew it well. When we had no one especially selected to "receive" in those days, it was a sort of garrison custom for everybody to present himself or herself to the wife of the commanding officer, in case that official was so provided. Mrs. Frazier was seated in plain view of the queenly creature who, having advanced a few steps beyond the portals and the loiterers there assembled, now halted, and like some finished actress swept the room with her radiant eyes, as though compelling all men, all women, to yield to her their attention and regard, and then, smiling brightly, beamingly (dutiful Brayton guided by the pressure of her daintily gloved hand), moved with almost royal grace and deliberation to where Mrs. Frazier sat in state; and the first lady of the garrison rose to greet her.

Unsuitable as is the full uniform for cavalry purposes to-day, it was worse in 1870, when our shoulders were decked with wabbly epaulets and our waists were draped with a silken sash that few men wore properly. But whatever might be said of Sir Galahad's shortcomings as a boon com-

panion, or of his severely simple and economical
mode of life, there was no manifestation of parsi-
mony in his attire. No man in the room was so
well uniformed, or wore the garb of his profession
with better grace. He who came in a flannel
shirt and a rough gray suit, with a silver watch
and leather watch-chain, appeared this night in
uniform of faultless cut and fit, with brand-new
glittering captain's epaulets, while his sash was of
the costliest silk net, of a brighter red than generally worn,—most officers appearing in a stringy
affair that age and weather had turned to dingy
purple. On his left breast Barclay wore the
badge in gold and enamel of a famous fighting
division in a gallant corps; and such badges were
rare in the days whereof I write. Moreover,
though neither a tall man nor a stalwart, Captain
Barclay was erect, wiry, and well proportioned,
and his head and face were well worth the second
look every one had been giving this night. "The
Twelfth have been swearing like pirates at having
another doughboy saddled on 'em," chuckled Captain Perkins, himself a doughboy. "Begad, the
Twelfth has no better picture of the officer and
the gentleman than this importation from the
Foot." But no one spoke with the thought of
being heard as Laura Winn finished her greeting
to Mrs. Frazier. Every man and woman was in-

tent only on what was coming next, although many strove to speak, or to appear to listen, to their neighbors. Charlotte Frazier actually rose from her seat and stepped out into the room that she might have a better view.

And Barclay would not have been the observant man he had already shown himself to be had he not known it. His color was a bit high for one whose face was ordinarily so pale, but he stood calmly erect, with an expression of pleased contemplation in his fine eyes, waiting for Mrs. Winn to finish the somewhat hurried yet lavish words that she addressed to Mrs. Frazier; then she turned effusively upon him.

"Captain Barclay!" she exclaimed. "How very good to see you here! and how glad we all are to welcome you to the Twelfth! Mr. Winn and I have been in despair because his illness has kept him a prisoner. Indeed, I doubt if I should have left him at all to-night but for his positive orders—and the doctor's; then, of course, I much wanted to see you—too."

She had begun confidently, even masterfully. She looked him with determined effort straight in the face at the start, but her confidence flitted before a dozen words were said. Her voice faltered before she had half finished, for Barclay's eyes frankly, even smilingly, met hers, and with

ease and dignity and courteous interest all com-
mingled he had bowed slightly over her hand,
lowered it after a brief, by no means lingering,
pressure, and stood, merely mentioning her name,
"Mrs. Winn," and, as was rather a way of his,
letting the other party do all the talking. It was
a godsend to Laura Winn that the waltz music
began at the next instant, for his nonchalance was
something utterly unexpected. Oh, how dared
he look so calmly, indifferently, forgetfully, almost unrecognizingly, into her eyes, and stand
there so placidly, when her heart was fluttering wildly with nervous excitement, her words
coming in gasps!

"Oh, Mr. Brayton, how heavenly!" she exclaimed. "Don't let us lose an instant of that
waltz." Over his glittering shoulder she beamed
in parting a bewitching smile, levelled all at Barclay, and glided away, a floating cloud of filmy
drapery, a vision of flashing eyes, of flushing
cheeks, of dazzling white teeth gleaming between
the parted rose-leaves of her mouth, of snowy
shoulders and shapely arms, of peeping, pointed,
satin-shod feet, the handsomest creature in all
that crowded room, and the most dismally unhappy. She had met him in the witnessing presence of all Fort Worth, and all the garrison saw
that she had sustained a crushing defeat. She

who was to have been his wife and had duped
him, she who had looked to subjugate him once
more, was duped in turn, the victim of her own
vanity.

"And to think," said Mrs. De Lancy, "she
only changed her half-mourning a month ago,
and now—in full ball costume!"

Fort Worth didn't stop talking of that episode
for all of another week, and that, too, in the face
of other interesting matter.

To begin with, Sergeant Marsden had disappeared as though from the face of the earth.
Whither he had fled no man could say. No set-
tlement worth the name had not been searched,
no ranch remained unvisited. Fuller's people
would not shield the fugitive, for Fuller, as the
post sutler, suffered equally with Uncle Sam from
the sergeant's depredations. Settlers and ranch
people who bought of the latter cut into the business of the former, and Fuller would most gladly
have had him "rounded up" long weeks ago; but
Marsden and his few confederates in the garrison
had admirably covered their tracks, and the indications of declining trade that had roused the sutler's suspicions led to no arousal of vigilance
within the sentry line: wherefore Fuller's heart
was hardened against the post commander and the
erstwhile commissary, and this, too, at a time

when the latter stood in sorest need of financial
help. The extent of poor Winn's losses and responsibility was now known: so far as his commissary accounts were concerned, not a cent less than
three thousand dollars would cover them. The
quartermaster was out a horse and equipments,
and several confiding enlisted men and laun-
dresses were defrauded of money loaned the dashing sergeant. Uncle Sam, be it known, has summary methods as a bill-collector. He simply stops
his servant's pay until the amount due is fully
met. Winn's total pay and emoluments as com-
puted in '70 and '71 would barely serve in two
years to square himself with his exacting Uncle.
Meantime, what were wife and baby and other
claimants to do? What was he to live on, and
so insure payment of which his death would de-
stroy all possibility? Crushed as Winn was, there
were men and women who roundly scored his
wife for appearing superbly dressed at the first
ball graced by the presence of her discarded
lover. Yet had she stayed away, their disappointment would have exceeded this disapprobation.
Collabone said his patient suffered from a low
fever, which the unprofessional found difficult to
understand, in view of Mrs. Winn's diagnosis,
which declared it alarmingly high. Certain it is
that he kept his room until four days after the

evening of the ball; then he had to turn out and face the music, for orders came from "San Antone."

Then, too, came another invoice of interesting matter to Fort Worth, and it must be remembered that, in the narrow and restricted life of the far frontier, interest existed in matters that seem too trivial for mention in the broader spheres of the metropolis. The invoice was an actual and material fact, and consisted of a big wagon-load of household goods consigned to Captain Barclay, accompanied by a dignified Ethiopian and two very knowing-looking horses that had many of the points of thoroughbreds. The quartermaster's train under proper escort had made the long pull from Department Head-Quarters, and all unannounced came these chattels to the new troop leader. The very next morning, which was a Sunday, when Brooks's four troops formed line for inspection in the old-fashioned full dress of the cavalry, the men in shell jackets and plumed felt hats, the officers in long-skirted, clerical-looking frock-coats, black ostrich plumes, gold epaulets, and crimson sashes, there rode at the head of Lawrence's old troop a new captain, whose horse and equipments became the centre of critical and admiring eyes the moment it was possible for his comrades to leave their commands and gather about him. Very few officers in those days possessed anything better than the regulation troop bridle and raw-hide McClellan saddle, which with their folded blankets satisfied all the modest requirements of the frontier. The light-battery-men indulged in a little more style and had picturesque red blankets to help out, but even they were put in the shade, and came trotting over during the rest after Brooks had made the formal ride round to look at the general appearance of his command. All hands seemed to gather in approbation about Barclay's charger. The horse himself was a bright, blooded bay, with jet-black, waving mane, tail, and forelock, superb head, shoulders and haunches, and nimble legs, all handsomely set off by a glistening bridle with double rein, martingale, glossy breast-strap and polished bits, curb-chain, bosses, rings, and heart, with the regimental number in silver on the bosses and at the corner of the handsome shab-raque of dark blue cloth, patent leather, and the yellow edging and trimming of the cavalry. "The only outfit of the kind at Worth," said Brooks, emphatically. "And yet, gentlemen," he continued, seeing latent criticism in the eyes of certain of the circle, "it's all strictly in accordance with regulations, and just as we used to have it in the old days before the war. I wish we all had the same now. I haven't seen a Grimsley outfit since '61."

"Grimsley it is," said the veteran captain of the light battery. "Mine went to Richmond in '61 with what we didn't save of our battery at First Bull Run."

"Grimsley it is," said his junior subaltern. "If Sam Waring could only see that, he'd turn green with envy to-day and borrow it to-morrow." Whereat there went up a laugh, for Waring was a man of mark in the queer old days of the army.

Then of course every one wanted to know, as the cavalcade rode from the drill-ground up to the post, where Barclay had bought his horses, and some inquired how much they cost; and to all queries of the kind Barclay answered, with perfect good humor, that he had ordered the equipments of the old firm of Grimsley, still doing business in St. Louis, as it did in the days when Jefferson Barracks and Leavenworth and Riley were famous cavalry stations in the '50s; the horses he had bought of a family connection in Kentucky, and had given seven hundred dollars for the pair.

"See here, Hodge," growled the old stagers as they clustered about the club-room, sipping cooling drinks after the warm morning exercise, "what's all this you've been telling us about Bar-

clay's inexpensive, economical, and skimpy ways?
He's got the outfit of a British field-marshal, by
gad!"

But Hodge was too much concerned and con-
founded to speak. "It's more'n I can explain,"
he said. "Why, he wouldn't spend ten cents in
Wyoming."

And yet, had Hodge only known it, Barclay's
infantry outfit was of just as fine finish and material, as far as it went, as these much more costly
and elaborate appointments of the mounted service. Everything connected with the dress or
equipments of his profession Barclay, who would
spend nothing for frivolities, ordered of the best
furnishers, and no man ever appeared on duty in
uniform more precise or equipments of better
make.

Of course the club-room was not the only place
where Barclay's really bewildering appearance
was discussed. Among the officers there were
many who growled and criticised. It was all
right to have handsome horses, if he could afford
it: any cavalryman would try to do that, was the
verdict. "But all these other jimcracks, they're
simply moonshine!" And yet, as pointed out by
Major Brooks, it was all strictly according to
regulation. "Damn the regulations!" said Captain Follansbee; "they're too expensive for me."

And, take it all in all, the feeling of the mess was rather against than with Barclay; he had no business wearing better clothes or using better horse-furniture than did his fellows. Follansbee went so far as to tackle Blythe on the subject and invoke his sympathy, but that massive old dragoon disappointed him. "Barclay's right," said he; "and if the rules were enforced we'd all have to get them."

"But they cost so much," said Follansbee.

"Not half what you spend in whiskey in half the time it would take to get them here," was the unfeeling rejoinder.

Mrs. Frazier and Mrs. De Lancy, however, wished the captain had brought an easy open carriage with driving horses instead of saddlers. It would have been far more useful, said those level-headed women. And so it might have been—to them.

But in the midst of all the talk and discussion came tidings that amazed Fort Worth. Ned Lawrence was actually on his way back to Texas,—would be with his precious babies within the fortnight,—would reoccupy his old quarters for a while at least as the guest of the usurper, for they had been formally chosen by Captain Barclay, to the frantic wrath of Ada when first she heard the news,—wrath that sobbed itself out in the lap of her loving friend Mrs. Blythe, as the motherless girl listened with astonished ears to the explanation.

"So far from raging at him, Ada, you should be thankful that your dear father and you and Jimmy have found so thoughtful and generous a friend as Captain Barclay. If he had not chosen your house, Captain Bronson would have done so, and you would have had to go. As it is, nothing of yours or your father's will be disturbed."

And sorely tempted was the enthusiastic, tender-hearted woman to tell much more that, but for his prohibition, she would have told; and yet she did not begin to know all.

CHAPTER VII.

WITHIN the fortnight came poor Ned Lawrence back to Worth, and men who rode far out on the Crockett trail to meet the stage marvelled at the change three months had made in him. He had grown ten years older, and was wrinkled and gray. Winn was of the party, and Winn, who a month gone by was looking haggard, nervous, miserable, now rode buoyantly, with almost hopeful eyes and certainly better color than he had had for months, despite the fact that he had lost both flesh and color during his illness. Something had happened to lighten his load of dread and care. Something must have happened to enable Lawrence to take that long, long journey back to Texas. Fort Worth indulged in all manner of theories as to where the money was coming from, and Barclay, of course, was suspected, even interrogated. The frankest man in some respects that ever lived, Captain Galbraith Barclay was reticent as a clam when he saw fit to keep silent, and men found it useless to question or women to hint. As for Winn, he had but one classmate at the post, Brayton, who had never been one of his intimates at the Point, and, being rather, as was said, of the "high and mighty," reserved and distant sort with the subalterns he found at Worth on joining three winters before, Winn had never been popular. Lawrence was his one intimate, despite the disparity in years. And so no man ventured to ask by what means he expected to meet the demands thus made upon him. The board of survey ordered to determine the amount of the loss and fix the responsibility had no alternative. Winn and his few friends made a hard fight, setting forth the facts that the count had been made every month as required by orders and regulations, and that except by bursting open every bale, box, and barrel, and sifting over the contents, it would have been impossible to detect Marsden's methods. On some things the board was disposed to dare regulations and raps on the knuckles, and to let Winn off on several others; but what was the use? "the proceedings would only be sent back for reconsideration," said their president; and as it transpired that Winn had not exercised due vigilance, but had trusted almost entirely to his sergeant, they decided to cut the Gordian knot by saddling the young officer with the entire responsibility, which meant, sooner or later, a stoppage of nearly three thousand dollars of his pay.

It is a sad yet time-honored commentary at the expense of human nature that the contemplation of the misfortunes of our fellow-men is not always a source of unalloyed sorrow. There was genuine and general sympathy for Lawrence, because he had been poor and pinched and humbled for years, had worn shabby clothes, and had sought all possible field duty, where "deeds, not duds," as a garrison wit expressed it, seemed to make the man. He had frankly spoken of his straits and worries to such as spoke to him in friendship, and this, with his deep and tender love for his children, and his capital record as a scout leader, had won over to him all the men who at one time were envious and jealous and had cherished the linesman's prejudice against the fellow whose duties for years had kept him on the staff. The women were all with him, and that meant far more than may seem possible outside the army. There was many a gentle dame in the old days of adobe barracks who could be an Artemisia in the cause of a friend.

No one knew just what object Ned Lawrence had in coming back to Dixie. Every one knew he had indignantly refused the second lieutenancy, despite the fact that one or two men with war service and rank almost equal to his own had meekly accepted the grudgingly tendered com-

mission, and others were said to be about to follow suit,—all, presumably, with the hope that
their friends and representatives in Congress assembled would speedily legislate them back where
they thought they belonged. No one knew where
Ned Lawrence had made a raise of money, but
raise he certainly had made, for, to Blythe's indignation, there came a draft of one hundred dollars to cover the expenses, he said, of his children
and old Mammy and to pay the latter some of
her wages. The balance he would settle, he
wrote, when he arrived. Blythe would far rather
he had waited until his accounts were adjusted;
then, if Lawrence were in funds, Blythe could
have found no fault with this insistence on at
least partially defraying the expenses incurred in
providing for the little household. Lawrence
hoped to have his accounts adjusted, his letter
said, and he had reason to believe, from what
friends in Washington told him, that he would
find his successor willing to receipt to him for
missing items, trusting to luck and the flotsam
and jetsam of the frontier to replace them in
course of time. Lawrence, indeed, was curious
now to meet and know Captain Barclay, for he
had been told many things that had gone far to
remove the feeling of unreasoning antagonism he
had felt at first.

Only one thing did he say to Blythe that threw light on his future plans. "I am dreadfully sorry," he wrote, "to hear such ill tidings about Harry Winn. I was always fearful there was something wrong about that fellow Marsden, and sometimes strove to caution him,—I, who could not see the beam in my own eye,—I, with two scoundrels in my orderly-room, trying to warn him against the one in his! Winn is a proud, sensitive, self-centred sort of fellow, whom wealth perhaps might have made popular. He is no better manager than I. He has a wife who could never help him to live within his means, as poor Kitty certainly tried to do with me." (Oh, the blessed touch of Time! Oh, the sweet absolution of Death! Kitty was an angel now, and her ways and means were buried with all that was mortal of her.) "And, worse than all, poor Hal has no one, I fear, to help him now, as—I write it with blinded eyes, dear Blythe—it has pleased God I should find in many friends in the days of my sore adversity,—you and your blessed wife, and the colonel, and Brooks,—even rough old Follansbee and our dilettante De Lancy, and that inimitable Collabone. My heart overflows, and my eyes, too, at thought of all you and they have done and said and written for me and mine. And here, too, where in my bitterness I thought I was

deserted of all, here is gallant old Front de Bœuf
(you remember how we swore by him in the Valley after Davy Russell was killed). He has
housed and fed and nursed and cared for me like
a brother, and Senator Howe and even old Catnip
—God bless him!—have worked hard for me;
and, though my soldier days seem over for the
time at least, my stubborn spirit has had to surrender to such counsellors and friends as they
have been to me. They all say Congress will
surely put me back next winter, and meantime
'Buffstick' says I'm to have a salaried position in
a big company with which he is associated, and to
begin work as soon as my health is re-established
and my accounts straightened out."

"Who is Buffstick?" queried Mrs. Blythe, at
this juncture.

"Buffstick? Oh, that was our pet name for
Colonel Dalton, of the —th Massachusetts, Lawrence's friend and host in Washington; a magnificent fellow, dear, with a head and chest that
made some lover of Scott liken him to Front de
Bœuf,—out of 'Ivanhoe,' you know. But he was
a stickler for neatness in dress and equipments,
and his regiment called him Buffstick, and grew
to love him all the same. He commanded a brigade after Cedar Creek, and now,—just think of
it!—he's a capitalist."

"Does he know Captain Barclay, do you think?" she asked, after a reflective pause.

"I'm sure I don't know. Probably not," was the answer. "They never served in the same part of the army. Why do you ask?"

"Oh, I was wishing—I couldn't help thinking —how much Mr. Winn needed some good friend, too."

"Winn and Lawrence are very different men," said Blythe, gravely. "Lawrence has made friends, while poor Winn has only enemies, I fear, and, really, none worse than himself."

Mrs. Blythe sighed as she turned away. It was much as her husband said. The Winns had come to the regiment after a round of receptions, dinners, and dances in their honor all the way from Washington to Worth, and had "started with a splurge," as the chroniclers declared. Laura's gowns and airs and graces won her no end of prominence, but very few friends. Winn's "high and mighty" ways, so they were termed by all the garrison, in which at that time only two or three West Pointers could be found, had alienated all the subs, most of the seniors, and many of the women. Their extravagance during the first year of service, the explanations and excuses tendered by Laura in the next, and Harry's increasing moodiness and distraction, served only

to widen the breach. Men and women both, who
began by envying, turned to openly decrying.
Cutting things were said to Laura, whose men-
dacities provoked them. Sneering or at least suggestive things were often said in presence of
Winn, if not exactly to him; for there was one
quality about the swell the garrison had to respect,—his cheerful and entire readiness to fight
on very small provocation, and those were the
days when the tenets of the "code" were not
totally forgotten, and there still remained in the
army a sentiment in favor of the doctrine of personal responsibility for disparaging words. There
would be fewer courts-martial to-day were there
more of it left. But when women heard the
stories about the big bill at the sutler's and others
that came by mail, and made little icy comments
about some people being able to afford much more
than *they* could, Laura laughed off the allusions
to their superior style of living by stories of an
indulgent papa, until papa's death left her without further resource from that quarter. Then she
set afloat a fabrication about a doting aunt of
Harry's who had no children of her own,—an
amiable old widow who was to leave him all her
money. He did have an aunt of that description,
but she didn't have the money, and there were
men who were malicious enough to refer in

Winn's presence to their wish that they had wealthy fathers-in-law or doting dowager aunts, thereby giving some other fellow a chance to say, "And so does Fuller, no doubt."

Indeed, so practically friendless were the Winns that among nine out of ten families along officers' row there was a feeling of lively curiosity to note the effect of this supposably crushing blow on the unhappy pair, and a consequent sentiment, only partially veiled in many cases, of keen disappointment when the news flew around the garrison that Mr. Winn had announced his readiness to meet the demand in full.

"Why, it can't be true," said many a woman. "I'll believe it when I see the money," said many a man. "Do you suppose—he could have accepted it from—Captain Barclay?" asked, in strictest confidence, Mrs. De Lancy of Laura's erstwhile intimate, Mrs. Faulkner.

"Not *Harry* Winn, probably," answered Mrs. Faulkner, in confidence equally inviolable, "but ——" and the pause that followed was suggestive. Follansbee and Bellows bolted down to the sutler's with the surprising news, wondering if Fuller could have been ass enough to advance the money. There was a time when he would have done so, perhaps, for he was one of the first to be enthralled by young Mrs. Winn's grace and

beauty, and lavished presents upon her—and
upon Winn, of course—for a month, until Winn
put a stop to the presents and Mrs. Fuller came
post-haste back from San Antonio and put a stop
to other manifestations.   But Fuller had long
since become estranged from the Winns,—the
presentation of his bill at inopportune times
having later widened the apparent breach.   His
jaw fell and his mouth opened wide when he
heard the news, for Fuller had begun to believe
that he would never get his money, and resented
it that Uncle Sam should be luckier.

   "Send up another 'bill rendered' by Ikey to
Mr. Winn this afternoon," he bade his clerk, as
the investigators departed to follow other clues.
Fuller had gone down into his pockets, unbe-
known to the post, and had actually pressed on
Lawrence a loan of three hundred dollars, and
bade him come for more when that was gone, but
not a cent would he put up for Harry Winn,—
not he; "the damned supercilious snob," was
what Fuller now called him, not so much because
he thought him a snob or supercilious or even de-
serving of damnation, as because he had allowed
himself to be robbed of three thousand dollars'
worth of goods that might otherwise have been
purchased of him, Fuller, for double or treble the
money.   No, plainly, Fuller was not the angel

that had come to the rescue of Winn, nor could
Follansbee or Bellows or the rest of the fellows
find out who had. The mystery of Gilgal was
outdone. Even Frazier and Brooks did not know,
and when some one, possibly Mrs. Frazier, suggested to the colonel that as the commanding officer he really ought to know, the colonel did send
for his new quartermaster and say to him, "Mr.
Trott, as you are to receipt to Mr. Winn for the
money value of his shortage, it would be well to
be very circumspect. He probably cannot have
that much in currency here. How does he propose to pay it?"

"I don't know, sir," said the man of business,
promptly. "He says he will be ready to cover the
entire amount on or before the 20th of May. I
didn't like to ask him where it was to come from."

Neither did Frazier, despite no little prodding
at home. Only one man ventured to speak of it
to Winn, and, the resultant conversation having
been variously and exaggeratively reported, the
truth should here be told. It was at the club-
room, which, for the first time in weeks, Mr.
Winn entered. He asked for Major Brooks, and,
finding him absent, turned to go out with no
more than a nod to the party at the poker-table.
That party was made up mainly of the class that
was numerous in the army in those days and is

as rare as an Indian fight now. The least responsible among them at the moment was Lieutenant Bralligan, ex-corporal of dragoons, who
could no more have passed the examination ex-
acted of candidates to-day than a cat could squeeze
through a carbine. "Ilwat d'ye warrnt of the
meejor, Winn?" he shouted. "Sure ye've got
permission to ride out wid us to meet Lawrence."

Winn vouchsafed no answer. Bralligan and
he were things apart, a reproach to each other's
eyes, and the evil blood in the Irishman, inflamed
already by whiskey, boiled over at the slight.
"It's Barclay ye're looking for, not Brooks!" he
shouted, in tempestuous wrath. "Faith, if ye
want anything out o' the Quaker, let yer wife do
the——"

Instantly a brawny hand, that of Captain Follansbee, was sprawled over the broad, leering
mouth. Instantly there was a crash of chair-legs
hastily moved, of grinding boot-heels as men
sprang to their feet, of poker-chips flying to the
floor,—a sound of oaths and furious struggles, for
two of the party, with the attendant, had hurled
themselves on the half-drunken lieutenant and
were throttling him to silence, while Captains
Bronson and Fellows sprang to head off Winn,
who with blazing eyes and clinched fists came
bounding back into the room.

"What did that blackguard say?" he demanded. "I did not catch the words."

"Nothing, nothing, Winn, that you should notice," implored Bronson. "He's drunk. He doesn't know what he is saying. He's crazed. No, sir," insisted Bronson, sternly, as Winn strove to pass him. "If you do not instantly withdraw I shall place you under arrest. Be sure that this poor devil shall make all reparation when he's sober enough to realize what has happened. Go at once.—You go with him, Fellows."

And so between them they got Winn away, and others soused Bralligan with *acequia* water and locked him up in his room and had him solemnly sober by afternoon stables, while, vastly to their relief, Winn with two or three cavaliers rode away at three o'clock to meet Ned Lawrence somewhere afar out on the Crockett trail. Greatly did Follansbee and Fellows congratulate Bronson, and Bronson them, on the fact that they had happened to be looking on at the game when Winn happened in and Bralligan broke out; for thereby they had stopped what might have been a most tremendous row. "All of which mustn't be known to a soul," said they.

But Bralligan's voice was big and deep. It was one of the causes of his unhallowed preferment in the days when second lieutenancies were showered on the rank and file the first year of the war. Bralligan's taunting words, only partially audible to Winn as he issued from the front of the building, were distinctly heard by domestics lying in wait for a chance to borrow of the steward and pick up gossip at the back. By stables that evening the story was being told high and low all over the post; even the children heard with eager yet uncomprehending ears; and so it happened that just as the drums of the infantry were sounding first call for retreat parade, and the women-folk were beginning to muster on the porches, and the warriors of the Foot along the opposite side at the barracks, and as Captain Barclay, a light rattan stick in his hand, came strolling back from stables, Lieutenant Brayton at his side, little Jim Lawrence made a dash from a group of children, and, in the full hearing of several officers and half a dozen women, a shrill, eager, childish voice piped out the fatal words,—

"Uncle Gal—Uncle Gal—what did Mr. Bwalligan mean by telling Mr. Winn to send his wife to you for money?"

Laura Winn herself was on the nearest piazza at the moment, stunningly handsome, and posing for a bow from her next-door neighbors as they came by. She and every other woman there distinctly heard the words and marked the effect.

Sir Galahad's face flushed crimson. He caught his little friend up in his arms and held him close to his burning cheek. "Hush, Jimmy boy. He meant nothing, and soldiers never repeat such nonsense. Run to sister Ada and help her get everything ready for papa's coming. Think, Jimmy, he'll be here by tattoo." And with a parting hug he set the youngster down at his door-step and started him on his way. Then, courteously raising his cap to the gathering on the nearest porch, and noting, as did they, that Mrs. Winn had disappeared within her hall, Barclay quickly entered his own portal, and nabbed Brayton as he was making a palpable "sneak" for the rear door. The youngster found escape impossible. Will he, nill he, the boy told the story as it had been told to him, Barclay standing looking straight into his eyes, as though reading his very soul, yet never saying a word beyond the original, "You heard what Jimmy said. It is another instance of 'out of the mouths of babes and sucklings,' Brayton. Now, tell me exactly what you know."

It was a warm May evening. A hot south-wester had been blowing from the broad valley of the Rio Bravo, and the few men in the club-room at nine o'clock were demanding cooling drinks. Bralligan was there, looking somewhat solemn and sheepish. He knew that nothing but the presence of senior officers had prevented a serious fracas as the result of his asinine bray that morning, but, now that Winn was out of the way and the matter in the hands of his captain, he had no dread of the thrashing he deserved, and was disposed to an exhibition of bravado. A drink or two added to his truculence, as well as to his desire to resume the game interrupted that morning. There were always in those days a few reliable gamblers at the big frontier posts, and presently Bralligan, in his shirt-sleeves, was contemplating a sizable pile of chips and bantering a burly captain to "see his raise," when suddenly he became aware of a distracted look in the eyes of the group about the table, and, glancing towards the door, his own blood-shot orbs lighted upon the trim figure of Captain Barclay, standing calmly surveying the party,—Barclay, who never smoked, drank, or played cards, and who was reported to have started a movement for prayer-meetings among the enlisted men. His very presence in that atmosphere was ominous, especially as the gaze of his usually soft brown eyes was fixed on Bralligan. One or two men said, "Good-evening, captain," in an embarrassed way, but the Irish subaltern only stared, the half-grin on his freckled face giving place to an uneasy leer.

On a bench to the left of the entrance stood a huge water-cooler, with gourds and glasses by its side. Underneath the spigot was a big wooden pail, two-thirds full of drippings and rinsings. Without a word, the new-comer stepped quietly within the room, picked up the bucket, and, striding straight to the table before Bralligan could spring to his feet, deftly inverted the vessel over the Irishman's astonished head, deluging him with discarded water and smashing the rim well down on his unprotected shoulders. An instant more, and Bralligan sent the bucket whirling at his assailant's head, which it missed by a yard, then, all dripping as he was, followed it in a furious charge. Sir Galahad "side-clipped" with the ease and nonchalance of long but unsuspected practice, and let fly a white fist which found lodgement with stunning crash straight under the Irishman's ear, felling him like an ox.

CHAPTER VIII.

AND so Ned Lawrence got back to Worth to find it far livelier than when he left it. The stage with its joyous escort had come trundling in just before tattoo, and first and foremost the returning wanderer was driven to his own door-way and left for half an hour with Ada and Jimmy—the one sobbing with joy, the other laughing with delight—on the father's knees. Then Mrs. Blythe stole in to bid them to the waiting supper, and, pending Lawrence's reappearance somewhere along the line, the officers gathered in low-voiced groups discussing the startling event of the evening. Bralligan, raging for the blood of the double-dashed, triple-adjectived hound who had assaulted him, had been lugged home by two or three of his kind, consoled by Captain Mullane with the assurance that he'd see that the preacher gave him full satisfaction in the morning, for, with native love of a ruction, Mullane stood ready to bear the subaltern's challenge, even though his better nature told him the ducking was richly deserved: with Irish honor in question, Mullane was for fight.

108

Frazier and Brooks, of course, said the seniors present, must not be allowed official knowledge of what had taken place, though in those benighted days of magnificent distances from the centre of civilization and the exploring grounds of reporters of the press, many a stirring row was settled without its ever being heard of beyond the limits of the garrison in which it occurred. Captain Barclay, contenting himself with the one blow, despite an unchristian impulse to follow it up with a kick at the sprawling figure, had stood calmly by when Bralligan's associates lifted him, half stunned, to his feet, then, addressing himself to Mullane, with just the least tremor in his voice and twitching to his muscles, remarked, "Of course you know what led to this, sir. If your lieutenant desires to follow it up, you can find me at my quarters." Then, looking very deliberately around upon the little circle of flushed or pallid faces,—there were only five officers present,—he slowly turned, walked away, and shut himself in his room.

A light was still burning there when Brayton tiptoed in at half-past ten. He, with several other cavalrymen, had been sitting in the major's parlor, listening to Lawrence's tale of his experiences in Washington. Winn had rejoined the party late, and one glance at his face was enough

to tell Brayton that somewhere he had heard of
the fracas at the club-room. Brayton's boyish
heart was bubbling over with pride and delight in
this new and unlooked-for side to his captain.
Every day of his service with that officer only
served to strengthen the regard and admiration
Brayton felt for him. Barclay had made no pre-
tence of being a cavalryman on the strength of
his assignment to that arm. He started with the
assertion that he had everything to learn, and
then surprised his subaltern by an extensive
knowledge of what we then called "the tactics."
He was certainly not as much at home in saddle
as on foot, and did not pretend to be, but he was
by no means a poor or ungraceful rider. He had
a light, gentle hand, at least,—a thing much
harder for most men to acquire than a good seat.
He was very cool, just, and level-headed with the
members of the troop, not a few of whom thought
to "run it" on the "doughboy" captain; but all
such projects had flattened out within the fortnight after his coming. Barclay might not know
horses, but he did know men, and the first sergeant was the first to find it out,—the new captain calmly and almost confidentially pointing
out to him, after ten days of apparently casual
glancings over the mess-room and kitchen, that
the men were not getting their proper allowance

of coffee, and that the savings made on the rations did not all go where they belonged.

"Boy an' man, sorr," began Sergeant Sullivan, oratorically and with fine indignation, "I've sarved in the dragoons or cavalry the best fifteen years of me life, and this is the furrst time me honor's been called into account. I shall tindher me resignation at wanst."

"I have had its acceptance in contemplation for some days, sergeant," was the calm response. "But first we'll overhaul the accounts."

"Currnel Larns's, sorr, would niver have treated an ould soldier in this way."

"That, I fear, is true," was the imperturbable response, " and as a consequence the colonel appears to have been robbed right and left,—your own name being brought into question. That will answer for the present, sergeant."

And when the troop heard that Denny Sullivan had been "broke" and was to be tried by court-martial for thieving, great was the comment excited, and the men began to wonder what manner of doughboy was this, after all, that had come to them,—the doughboy that ould Denny had so confidently counted on running to suit himself. But this didn't begin to be all. A very acute trailer was Galahad. Those were days in which only a subaltern, and not always even a subaltern,

was expected to appear at morning stables; but
the new captain liked to rise early, he said. He
was up with the sun or earlier, and hoof- or wheel-
tracks about the stables before the herd was led
forth to water never escaped his attention, yet
apparently never excited remark. Within the
third week, however, another non-commissioned
officer was suddenly nabbed, and so was a wagon-
load of forage, going off to a neighboring ranch
at four o'clock in the morning. Meantime the
men noted that their coffee and rations were better and more bountiful, and soldiers are quick to
receive impressions that come by way of the
stomach. "The new captain is knocking out the
old abuses," said they, and it was wonderful how
soon the ex-doughboy made his way into their
good graces. There had been some disposition on
the part of the wits in other companies to refer
to Barclay's men as "The Parson's Own" when it
was announced that the captain had attended the
chaplain's evening service, but even that was beginning to die out, when all of a sudden it was
noised abroad this evening that the redoubtable
Bralligan had been felled by a single blow of that
Quaker fist.

Brayton was fairly quivering with excitement
this night of nights, and could not sleep. He
longed to see his captain and hear his version of

the affair, but the door was tightly closed instead of being invitingly open, and he dared not intrude. Not one word had been said about the matter at the major's, but Brayton knew it would soon be known even to the officer in command. So long, however, as it was not reported to him officially, Frazier would probably let the affair take its course. Bralligan deserved the knockdown, and doubtless would be glad enough to let the matter end there. But, thought Brayton, if he should demand satisfaction, and Barclay's religious or conscientious scruples were to prevent his acceptance, "*then* comes my chance," for the youngster himself proposed to take it up. He had no scruples. He had been longing for a chance to kick that cad Bralligan for over a year, and after all it was Barclay that got it.

Eleven o'clock, and Barclay's light still burned. Eleven-thirty, and still, reading or writing, the captain seemed occupied in the old poker room, and the door remained closed. Once or twice Brayton heard him moving about, and in his own excitement and interest the boy found it impossible to think of anything else. Twelve o'clock came. He was beginning to undress and prepare for bed, still uneasily watching the light shining through the crack of the door, when his straining ears caught the sound of a footfall underneath his

window. It opened on the yard, and the sill was
only five feet or so above the ground. A hand
was uplifted without and tapped gently on the
sash, and as Brayton drew aside the curtain Harry
Winn's face was revealed in the moonlight.

"Come to the porch in front," he muttered low.
"I must speak with you."

Brayton was out on the dark piazza in half a
minute. He found Winn nervously pacing the
boards.

"I told my wife I had to come out and think
quietly awhile," he said, as he extended a hand
to his silent classmate. "She heard of this—this
damnable business almost as quick as it happened.
That girl of ours hears everything and tells anything. There's no doubt about it, I suppose.
You were there? You heard it at once, didn't
you? What does—*he* say?" And Winn's nod
indicated that he meant Barclay.

"Nothing," said Brayton, briefly. "I haven't
seen him——"

"But he's up. The light's in his window.
He's writing—or something. Look here, Brayton, you know what's got to come of this. That
damned Irishman must challenge him, or be cut
and kicked about by all his kind in the cavalry.
It isn't Barclay's fight; it's mine. The more I
think of it the more I know that, contemptible a

blackguard as Bralligan is, he is still an officer of the regiment. He has been knocked down, and has the right to demand the only satisfaction there is for a blow. You know it as well as I do. What I've got to do right here and now is to take that fight off Barclay's hands, and you've got to help me."

"S'pose he don't want it taken off his hands," said Brayton, sturdily. "He told him plain enough he was ready to meet any demand——"

Winn reddened even in the pallid moonlight. "I say no man in this garrison-fights on my wife's account except me—or with me. They're up with Bralligan now, two or three of them, and I want you to go there with me at once as my witness. I mean to cowhide him to-night. Then if he wants a meeting in the morning, I'm his man." And as he spoke Winn thrashed nervously at the railing with the stout whip he carried in his hand.

"That won't fix it," answered Brayton, "and you ought to have sense enough to know it. Barclay has the precedence. The Mick couldn't challenge you until he'd fought him—or been refused a fight. You go to bed, Winn," and Brayton spoke even lower. "Your wife must have heard you just now, and first thing you know Barclay will hear you, and"—with almost comical irrelevance—"you don't want to meet him this way, when you haven't even called on him."

Winn reddened again. There was a tinge of bitterness in his tone as he answered,—

"Don't trouble yourself about Mrs. Winn's hearing. She's placidly asleep—long ago. As for my not calling, you know I've only been out of my bed three days or so, and Captain Barclay must understand that a man burdened as I have been is in no mood for social observances. This is all begging the question. You're the only man I can ask to be my second. Finish your dressing now and come."

"Winn, I won't do it," said Brayton, with flat-footed decision. "This is my captain's affair, and, from what I've seen of him since he joined, I'm bound to say what's his is mine. Besides, you've got no business mixing up in the matter. You've got your wife to think of, and you've got that commissary business to straighten out. Barclay and I have no encumbrances of either kind." At the moment, I fear me, the young gentleman could have added, "Thank God!" for, with all his appreciation of the physical perfections of his classmate's wife, Mr. Brayton was keenly aware of her many extravagances.

"Of course I've a wife," answered Winn, hotly. "It's because of her I feel bound to take this up.

As for that commissary money, every cent will be here to square the shortage, whether I am or not. I'll tell you what others—— No! I can't even tell you, Brayton. But an old friend of my father's has offered his help. Now, once more, will you come or not?"

"No, Winn. You know well enough I'd see you through if—— Hush! There's Mullane and some one else coming out of his quarters now."

"Then, by God! I'll go alone," exclaimed Winn, "and it's got to be done before they get away." And he would have gone springing down the steps, but Brayton seized and held him.

"For God's sake, Harry, be quiet to-night. Don't go near him. Quiet, man! Can't you see? Those fellows are coming this way now!"

True enough, Mullane and his companion, who had issued from the fourth set of quarters down to the left, turned northward the moment they reached the walk, the moonlight gleaming on the buttons of their uniform frock-coats, but the sight and faint sound of scuffling on Winn's porch seemed to attract their attention. They stopped as though to reconnoitre, and just then the front door of Brayton's hall opened wide, and, with the broad light at his back, Captain Barclay stepped quietly forth.

"Brayton," he said, "you left the door ajar,

and it was impossible not to hear the latter part of this conference.—Mr. Winn, I presume," he continued, with calm, courteous bow, as the two young men, unclasping, turned and faced him. "I infer that you purpose going to Mr. Bralligan's quarters—now. Let me urge that you do nothing of the kind. Brayton is right. I see that, late as it is, some of their party are moving this way. Pray remember that as yet this is entirely my affair."

There was no time for other answer than a bow, a mumbled word or two, an embarrassed acceptance of the hand extended by the captain. Just as he said, Mullane and his friend were coming rapidly up the walk. They passed the Winns' gate, entered that of Brayton, and then it appeared that Mullane's friend was the ubiquitous Hodge, that Mullane was manifestly in his glory, and that both were perceptibly in liquor.

"Gintlemen," said the doughty captain, halting at the foot of the steps and raising his forage-cap with magnificent sweep, "gintlemen, I am the beerer of a missige from me frind Mr. Bralligan. Have I the honor of addhressin' Captain Barclay?" Fondly did Mullane imagine that he impressed his hearers as did Sir Lucius O'Trigger; and much did he remind one of them, at least, of Captain Costigan of blessed memory.

"This is Captain Barclay," that gentleman answered, in low tones, with a smile of amusement at Mullane's grandiloquent prelude, yet stepping quickly forward to meet the envoys. Winn could not but note that the captain's movement accomplished at once two objects. It left him and Brayton in the shade; it kept Mullane and Hodge in the moonlight and off the steps. "Pardon my suggesting that a lady sleeps in the front room aloft there, and that you speak low, so as not to disturb her. Where is your message?"

This was trying. Mullane loved his chest tones as he did his whiskey. His low voice was apt to be thick and husky and unimpressive, and to-night he was over-weighted with the sense of the gravity and importance of his mission, if with nothing else.

"Sorr," he said, with another flourish of the cap, "in accordince with the practice of gintlemen in the old arrumy, I am the bearer of a verrbal missige——"

The Quaker captain had already amazed the old dragoon sergeants by the intricacy and extent of his knowledge of their manners and customs. Now came a surprise for the officers.

"Pardon my interrupting," he said. "I do not assume to instruct in such matters, but there is manifestly only one kind of message 'according to the customs of the old army,'" and here he smiled quietly, "that should come from Mr. Bralligan now, and it must come in writing. I decline to recognize any other." Here Brayton nudged Winn approvingly, but the subalterns maintained a decorous silence.

"I've niver hurr'd of a challenge being refused on that account," said Mullane, majestically, "and if me wurreds are not sufficient, here's me frind Mr. Hodge——"

"Your words are not brought into question, Captain Mullane, but the manner of your message is. Let your friend put it in writing, and it will be received. Good-night to you, sir."

And, to Mullane's utter amaze and confusion, quickly followed by an explosion of wrath, Captain Barclay coolly turned and walked withindoors.

"Hould on dthere!" cried Mullane, as he started to spring up the steps, but Brayton stepped in front of him, and Hodge nervously grabbed his arm. Neither knew much of the "code" of the old days, but each had learned that Barclay rarely made a mistake. Winn, too, tall and strong, stepped in front of the angry Irishman as he broke out into expletives. "No more of that here, captain," he cried, forgetful of any consideration of rank. "This noise will wake the

post. Rest assured your principal will get all
the fight he wants;" and then, with growing
wrath, for Mullane was struggling to come to the
steps, "so will you, by God, if you advance
another foot."

"Winn—Winn, for heaven's sake, I say!"
cried Brayton, seizing the uplifted arm. "Go
home, Mullane. Damn it, you're in no shape to
handle such a matter to-night. Go home, or I
swear I'll call the officer of the day. He's coming now!" he exclaimed; and it was true, for the
sound of excited voices had reached the adjoining
quarters, and out from the doorway, sashed and
belted, came the massive form of Captain Blythe,
his sabre clanking on the door-sill. Out, too,
from Winn's hallway shot a broad beam of light,
and hastening along the porch came a tall, graceful form in some clinging rose-tinted wrapper,
all beribboned and fluffy and feminine. The men
fell away and Mullane drew back as Mrs. Winn
scurried to her husband's side and laid her white
hand on his arm. Forth again on the other side
of Winn came Barclay, and his deep tones broke
the sudden silence.

"Captain Mullane, leave this spot instantly,"
he ordered, stern and low. "I'll answer to you in
the morning."

"Come out of this, Mullane," demanded

Blythe, striding in at the gate. "Delay one second, and I'll order you under arrest."

Up slowly went Mullane's cap with the same incomparable sweep. "In the prisince of leedies," said he, "I'm disarrumed. Captain Barclay, I'll see ye in the marrnin'."

But when the marrnin' came both Mullane and his principal, beside bewildering headaches, had graver matters to deal with than even a very pretty quarrel.

CHAPTER IX.

From the night of her brilliant appearance at the garrison ball, not once had Mrs. Winn an opportunity to exchange a dozen words with Captain Barclay. Her husband, as has been said, had failed to call on his new next-door neighbor, although Winn had been well enough to be about for several days, and until he did call it was impossible for Barclay to enter their doors, and expedient that he should avoid Mrs. Winn wherever it was possible to do so. This might not have been difficult, even though the same roof covered both households,—that of the Winns on the south and that of the Barclay-Brayton combination on the north side,—but for Laura Winn herself, who seemed to be out on the porch every afternoon as the captain came walking back from stables; and the women who were apt to gather at Mrs. Blythe's at that time declared that there was something actually inviting, if not imploring, in the way Mrs. Winn would watch for him, and bow, and seem to hover where he could hardly avoid speaking to her. Three times at least since that memorable party had she been there "on watch," as Mrs. Faulkner expressed it, **and** though his bow was courtesy itself, and his "Good-evening, Mrs. Winn," most respectful, and even kindly, if one could judge by the tone of his voice, not another word did he speak. He passed on to his own gateway, Brayton generally at his side, and his stable dress was changed for parade uniform or dinner before he again made his appearance.

After the manner of the day, most of the cavalry contingent stopped in at the club-room on the way back from evening stables. Brayton used to do so, but, though no one could say his captain had preached to him on the subject, some influence either of word or of example had taken effect, and the young bachelor seemed entirely content to cut the club and the social tipple, and to trudge along by his new companion's side. They had been getting "mighty thick" for captain and second lieutenant, said some of the other officers; but, serenely indifferent to what others thought or said, the two kept on their way.

"Thought you were goin' to wear mournin' for Lawrence the rest of your natural life, Brayton; and here you are tyin' to Barclay as if Lawrence had never lived," said Mr. Bralligan, only a day or two before Lawrence's return, and Brayton started almost as though stung. What Bralligan said was not half as ill grounded as most of his statements, and Brayton was conscious of something akin to guilt and self-reproach. In common with most of the regiment, he had felt very sore over Lawrence's going. He had been much attached to that gallant and soldierly captain, but now that another had taken his place, and he could compare or contrast the two, the youngster began to realize with something like a pang of distress—as though it were disloyal to think so— that in many ways Barclay was "head and shoulders" the superior man. Lawrence never rose till eight o'clock except when in the field. Lawrence rarely read anything but the papers and interminable controversies over the war. Lawrence, despite the claims of Ada and little Jimmy, often spent an evening at the club, and always stopped there on his way from stables. Lawrence never studied, and off the drill-ground never taught. Indeed, almost all the drills the troop had known for months and months Brayton himself had conducted. No wonder the boy had wasted hours of valuable time. No wonder there was a little game going on among the youngsters in Brayton's "back parlor" many a day. He had simply been started all wrong.

But even before Barclay's books were unpacked

the new captain had found means to interest the young fellow in professional topics that Lawrence had never seemed to mention. Barclay had evidently been taking counsel with progressive soldiers before joining his new regiment, had been reading books of their choosing, and among others was a valuable treatise on the proper method of bitting horses, and he found that here was a matter that Lawrence and Brayton had never thought of and that Brayton said was never taught them at the Point,—which was strictly true. To the amaze and unspeakable indignation of Denny Sullivan, who was soon to be overhauled on graver points, the doughboy had taken his lieutenant from horse to horse in the troop as they stood at rest during drill, and shown him at least twenty bits out of the forty-five in line that were no fit at all. He showed him some that were too broad from bar to bar and that slid to and fro in the tortured creature's mouth; others that hung too low, almost "fell through;" others whose curb-chain or strap, instead of fitting in the groove, bore savagely on the delicate bones above it and tormented the luckless charger every time his rider drew rein. Barclay gave the boy his own carefully studied hand-book; not another cavalry officer then at Worth had read it, though several had heard of it. The youngster was set to work fitting new bits by measurement to the mouth of every horse in the troop.

Then Barclay drew him into the discussion. of the cavalry system of saddling as then prescribed, —the heavy tree set away forward close to the withers,—and Brayton could only say that "that was tactics and the way they'd always done it." But Galahad pointed out that the tactics then in use were written of a foreign dragoon saddle with a long flat bearing surface. It was all very well for that to be set as far forward as it would go, because even then the centre of gravity of the rider would be well back on the horse. "But," said he, "you take this short McClellan tree, place that away forward, and then set a man in it; his centre of gravity will rest in front of the centre of motion of the horse,—will throw the weight on the forehand and use up his knees and shoulders in no time." This, too, set Brayton to studying and thinking, while Mullane and Fellows declared Sir Galahad a crank, and even Brooks and Blythe, wedded to tradition, thought him visionary. Then when the books came, Galahad unpacked, and just where the poker-table used to stand it stood now, but it was covered with beautiful maps of Alsace and Lorraine, and Galahad's desk with pamphlets sent him from abroad, the earliest histories of the memorable

campaign about Metz and Sedan. The next
thing Brayton knew he was as deeply interested
as his captain, and, lo, other men came to look
and wonder and go off shaking their heads,—
those of them who were of the Mullane persua-
sion sneering at those "book-generals," while
others, like Blythe, pulled up a chair as invited
and followed the junior captain through his
modest explanation with appreciative eyes.
Those were days when there was all too little time
for study and improvement, thanks to the almost
incessant Indian scouting required; but here was
Worth, a big post, and here was a four-troop battalion with a gentleman and not a bad soldier at
its head, and it had not occurred to him to teach
them anything or to require of them anything
beyond the usual attention to stables, troop-drill,
and an occasional parade. If his men were
reasonably ready to take the field in pursuit of
Kiowa, Comanche, or horse-thief, and to furnish
escort for ambulance and train when the disbursing officers went to and fro, that was all that could
be expected of him or them in those halcyon days.
And now "this blasted doughboy substitute" had
come down here and was proposing to stir them
all up, make them all out "so many ignoramuses,"
said Mullane. "Bedad, the thing is revolution-
ary!" And that was enough to damn it, for revo-

lution is a thing no Irishman will tolerate, when he doesn't happen to be in it himself.

Still another thing had occurred to make Barclay something apart from the bachelors. No sooner had his modest kit of household goods arrived than the unused kitchen of Brayton's quarters was fitted up; Hannibal was ensconced therein; a neat little dining-room was made of what had been designed for a small bedchamber on the ground-floor, and Barclay amazed the mess by setting forth champagne the last evening he dined there as a member, and then retired to the privacy of his own establishment, as he had at Sanders. The Winns' house-maid had of course dropped in to see how Hannibal was getting along, and dropped out to tell her discoveries, which were few. Then Brayton found the mess saying things about Barclay he could not agree with, and he, too, resigned and became a mess-mate of his captain,—a change for the better that speedily manifested itself in the healthy white of his clear eyes and a complexion that bore no trace of fiery stimulants such as were indulged in elsewhere. Then there was talk of others leaving the "Follansbee family" and asking to join at Brayton's, and this gave umbrage to Erin as represented in the bachelors' mess. And so an anti-Barclay feeling had sprung up at the post, among

the unlettered at least, and these were days in
which the unlettered were numerous. "Sorry
for you, Brayton, me boy," grinned the senior
sub of Fellows's troop. "It must be tough to
come down to this after Lawrence." And he was
amazed at Brayton's reply.

"Tough? Yes, for it shows me how much time
I've wasted."

"Wait till we get Galahad out on the trail
wid his new-fangled bits and seats," sneered
Mullane but a day or two before. "That'll take
the damned nonsense out of him. Faith, whin
he goes I hope I may go along too to see the fun."

And, sooner than he thought for, the Irish captain had his wish.

One o'clock had just been called off by the
sentries, and the moon was well over to the west,
when the door of the major's quarters was opened
and he with his lingering guests came forth upon
the broad piazza, the red sparks of their cigars
gleaming anew as they felt the fan of the rising
breeze. Clear and summer-like as was the sky,
there was a reminder of the snow-peaks in the
wings of the wind, and Lawrence huddled his old
cavalry cape about his shoulders as he faced it.
He was talking eagerly, perhaps a little bombas-
tically, of this great new mining company in
which Buffstick was prominent as a director. He

was full of hope and anticipation and disposed
to patronize a trifle his friends who, wedded to
the humdrum of the army, were debarred from
so fine an opportunity of making money in abundance. So many of the number were going to
do so much in the same way when first they left
us for the broader paths of civil life.

"I tell you, Brooks," he said, enthusiastically,
"I wouldn't take ten thousand dollars cash this
night for my chance of making twice that sum
within the year. Buffstick turns everything he
touches into gold."

"Wonder if Barclay knows these mines," said
De Lancy, reflectively, flipping the ashes from the
end of his cigar. "He has never opened his head
about his mines to a soul. We don't know where
they are."

"I don't know," said Lawrence, briefly. Even
yet the mention of Barclay chafed him a bit. "I
know this, though, that that company wouldn't
offer me any such salary as twenty-five hundred
dollars a year just to boss their men, unless there
was big money in it somewhere. It's the first
time I ever knew what it was to be indifferent to
the coming of the paymaster. By the way, he
ought to be here day after to-morrow, or to-morrow night in fact; it's long after twelve now.
The escorts were warned as we came along."

"I think it a mistake," said Brooks, gravely, "to let any one know beforehand when the paymaster is to start. That Friday gang probably musters a hundred by this time. It's where all our thieves and deserters go. I haven't a doubt your old sergeant has joined them by this time, Lawrence. I believe that's where Marsden's gone, and that we'll hear from them in force again before we're a month older. They've kept reasonably quiet all winter, but June isn't far off. I'm blessed if I would want to make that trip from San Antonio with forty thousand dollars in greenbacks with less than a big troop of cavalry to guard it."

"He's got more money than that this time," said Lawrence. "Most of these men have four months' pay due them; so have the cavalry along the route. He has two other posts to pay. Hallo!" he cried, breaking suddenly off, "what's all the light about down at the sutler's? Here comes the sergeant of the guard."

Running diagonally across the parade, the moonlight glinting on his buttons and accoutrements, an infantry non-commissioned officer was speeding towards the quarters of Captain Blythe, near the upper end of the row; but, catching sight of the group at the major's, he suddenly swerved and came straight towards them, spring-

ing over the gurgling *acequia* and the dusty roadway and halting at the gate.

"What is it, sergeant?" asked two or three
voices at once.

"I was looking for the officer of the day, sir.
Is he here?"

"Over at his quarters, probably. What's
amiss?"

"There's two of Fuller's men in, sir, from
Crockett,—just about played out. They swear
that not an hour after sunset the whole Friday
gang—it couldn't have been anything else—
came a-riding out from the foot-hills over towards
the Wild Rose and kept on to the southeast.
They saw the dust against the sky and hid in the
rocks away off to the east of the trail, and they
swear there must have been fifty of 'em at least."

He had hardly time to finish the words when
the sutler himself came galloping over the parade,
"hot foot," on his wiry mustang, and drew up in
front of the gate. "Has the sergeant told you?"
he asked, breathlessly. "It's Reed and his partner,—two of the best men on my ranch,—and
they can't be mistaken. You know what it must
mean, gentlemen. The gang is after the paymaster, and I think Colonel Frazier should know
at once." No wonder Fuller was breathless, bare-
headed, and only half dressed. Anywhere from

thirty to forty thousand dollars might be diverted
from its proper and legitimate use if that Friday
gang should overpower the guard and get away
with it. His coffers were filled with sutler checks
redeemable in currency at the pay-table, as was
the wonted way of the old army. It was a case
of feast or famine with Fuller, and he poured his
tale into sympathetic ears. Brooks himself went
over to the colonel's, and found that weasel of a
chief already awake. Mrs. Frazier didn't allow
galloping over her parade in the dead of the night
without an attempt to detect the perpetrator.
That vigilant dame had more than once brought
graceless skylarkers to terms, and the *quadrupe-
dante putrem sonitu* of Fuller's mustang represented to her incensed and virtuous ears only the
mad lark of some scapegrace subaltern, who per-
chance had not been as attentive to 'Manda as he
should have been, and she was out of dreamland
and over at the window before Fuller fairly drew
rein.

"What is it, Brooks, me boy?" asked Frazier
from his casement, as did gallant O'Dowd of his
loyal Dobbin. "I'll be down in a minute." By
the time he reached the door Fuller had hurried
up his stiff and wearied scouts, and in the presence
of a little party of officers the story was told again,
and told without break or variation. There was

only one opinion. The scattered outlaws had easily got wind of the coming of the paymaster with his unusual amount of treasure, and, quickly assembling, they were heading away to meet him far to the southeast of the big post, very possibly planning to ambuscade the party in the winding defiles of the San Saba Hills. Not a moment was to be lost. For the first time the full weight of his divorce from all that was once his profession and his pride fell on Ned Lawrence, as for an instant the colonel's eyes turned to him as of old, —the dashing and successful leader of the best scouts sent from Worth in the last two years. Then, as though suddenly realizing that he had no longer that arm to lean on, old Frazier spoke:

"Why, Brooks, you'll have to go. I can't trust such a command to Mullane, and it'll take two companies at least."

And twenty minutes later, answering the sharp summons of their veteran sergeants, the men of Mullane's and Barclay's troops were tumbling out of their bunks and into their boots, "hell-bent for a rousin' ride," and the old captain of Troop "D" was saying to the new, "Captain Barclay, may I ask you for a mount? I've been longing for two years past for a whack at this very gang, and now that the chance has come I cannot stay here and let my old troop go."

And all men present marked the moment of hesitation, the manner of reluctance, before Barclay gravely answered, "There is nothing at my disposal to which you are not most welcome, Colonel Lawrence; and yet—do you think—you ought to go?"

"I could not stay here, sir, and see my old troop go without me," was the answer.

Few were the families at Fort Worth that were not up and out on the piazzas or at the windows to see Brooks's detachment as it marched away in the light of the setting moon just as the stars were paling in the eastern sky; but the merciful angel of sleep spread her hushing wings over the white bed where two children lay dreaming, and never until the troopers were miles beyond the vision of the keen-eyed sentries did Ada know that the loved father, restored to her but a few hours before, was once more riding the Texan trail, soldier sense of duty leading on, and God alone knowing to what end.

CHAPTER X.

THE day that broke on old Fort Worth thus
late in a sunshiny May proved one of deep
anxiety. There was no telegraph wire then to
connect it with the distant head-quarters of the
department. If there had been it would have
been cut six times a week. There was no way of
waving back the coming convoy or of signalling
danger. Crockett Springs lay a long day's ride
to the southeast, and the little troop of cavalry
there in camp was looking for the coming of no
call upon it for duty until early on the morrow
it should supply the paymaster and his party with
breakfast, the ambulance with fresh mules and
driver, and the night riders of the escort with
their relief. Forty troopers from Crockett
Springs would take the place of those who had
come from the San Saba, and trot along with the
paymaster until, somewhere about midway to
Worth, they should meet the forty sent out the
previous night to bivouac on the prairie and be
ready to take up the gait and keep it until the
man of money and his safe were well within the
limits of the reservation. But the fifty-mile stage

from Crockett to the southeast was the worst on the long line. The road wound over the divide to the valley of the San Saba, and on the way had to twist and turn through defiles of the range of hills, where more than a dozen times Indians and outlaws had defied the little detachments of cavalry scouting after them. The worst part of the pass lay some twenty miles beyond the stage station at Crockett Springs. Neither Indians nor outlaws, to be sure, had been heard of in that neighborhood for several months, but that proved nothing. It was easy for the latter to sweep from their supposed fastnesses in the Apache range to the west, and, issuing from the Wild Rose Pass, to water miles below the springs and then line the rocks in the heart of the San Saba Pass, without a trooper being the wiser. Forty cavalrymen, as Lawrence knew, would be the major's escort from the camp on the Rio San Saba beyond the range. Forty men disciplined and organized ought ordinarily to be able to cope with any band of outlaws to be found in Texas. But when, as was now reasonably certain, this far-famed Friday gang had received accessions from the troops themselves and had welcomed the deserters and desperadoes so frequently sloughed off from the soldier skin of Uncle Sam in the days close following the great war, there was grave reason for precaution, and graver still for anxiety. Question as he might, Frazier could not shake an atom of the original statement of Fuller's men. Fifty mounted outlaws, at least count, with a dozen led horses, they had seen through their field-glass far over the prairie, pushing southeastward from the direction of Wild Rose Pass of the Apache range, straight for the lower valley through which ran the little stream that had its source at Crockett Springs.

So there were anxious hearts at Worth, for, while it was felt that Brooks would lose no moment and was well on his way at four o'clock of this bright Sunday morning, he had still some sixty miles to traverse before he could get to Crockett, rest and bait his men and horses, pick up Cramer's troop there camped, and then push ahead for the San Saba, where he expected to find the outlaw gang disposed in ambuscade, confidently awaiting the coming of their prey.

Now, Brooks had men enough to thrash them soundly, but unless he caught them in the act of spoliation he lacked authority. Just as sure as he pitched into a force of armed frontiersmen, they would appeal to the courts, and public sentiment would be dead against him. He could doubtless push ahead through the range, careless of lurking scouts of the would-be robbers, meet Major Pennywise and his protectors, and escort them

back in safety. That problem presented no great
difficulty; but what Frazier wanted and Brooks
wanted and everybody, presumably, wanted was
that the outlaws should be caught in the act and
be punished then and there. The question was
how to catch them in the act without being themselves discovered, and before the gang had had
time to inflict much damage on the paymaster's
party. There was the rub. "Why, their first
volley, delivered from ambush, might kill half the
outfit and the paymaster too," said Frazier. "No,
we dare not risk it, Brooks. Push through and
pull him through, that's the best we can do—unless," and here came the redeeming clause, "unless on the way you should light on some unforeseen chance. Then—use your discretion."

Mounted on the very horse he used to ride as
troop commander, and with the old familiar horse-
equipments, Ned Lawrence left the post at the
major's side. He had slept as only soldiers can,
curled up in the stage-coach, during the previous
afternoon, and was in far better trim for the long
ride in saddle than Captain Mullane, who with
bleary eyes and muddled head rode *solus* in front
of the leading troop, his one lieutenant, Mr. Bralligan, being reported by Dr. Collabone's assistant
as sick in quarters, which indeed he was, with a
lump the size of an apple on the side of his head,

and another, apparently the heft and density of a six-pounder cannon-ball, rolling about inside of it. "D" Troop, jogging easily along at the rear of column, was led by Barclay and Brayton, both of whom had marked the absence of the subaltern of the leading company, and neither of whom was surprised when ten miles out there came galloping past them, with a touch of the hand to his hat-brim, the late regimental commissary, Lieutenant Harry Winn.

"That's good!" said Brayton, as he saw his classmate ride up to the major and report, then fall back and range himself alongside Mullane. But Barclay was silent.

"You think he ought not to have come?" asked Brayton, half hesitatingly, as he glanced at his silent leader.

"I'm thinking more of others—who should be here," was the answer. "Yet those two have so much to leave." And Brayton, following the glance of his captain's eyes, fully understood.

The morning grew warm as the sun began to climb above the distant low-lying hills to the east. The dust soon rose in dense clouds from beneath the crushing hoofs, and, leaving Brayton with the troop, Barclay cut across the chord of a long arc in the trail and reined up alongside the major. The command at the moment was moving at a

sharp trot through a long, low depression in the
prairie-like surface.   Brooks returned the captain's punctilious salute with a cheery nod and
cordial word of greeting.

"With your permission, sir, I will fall back a
hundred yards or so, divide the troop into sections, and so avoid the dust."

Brooks glanced back over his shoulder. "Why,
certainly, captain," said he. "I ought to have
known the dust would be rising by this time.
It's eight o'clock," he continued, glancing at his
watch.   Barclay turned in saddle and signalled
with his gauntlet, whereat Brayton slackened
speed to the walk, and a gap began to grow between the rearmost horses of Mullane's troop and
the head of "D's" already dusty column.

"Ride with us a moment, won't you, Barclay?"
called the major, significantly, as his subordinate
seemed on the point of reining aside to wait for
his men. "I want you two to know each other."
And the new and the old captain of "D" Troop,
who had courteously shaken hands with each
other when presented in the dim light of the declining moon at four o'clock, now trotted side by
side, Lawrence eying his successor with keen yet
pleasant interest. He had been hearing all manner of good of him during the wakeful watches of
the night, and was manfully fighting against the

faint yet irrepressible feeling of jealous dislike
with which broader and better men than he have
had to struggle on being supplanted. Do what
he might to battle against it, Lawrence had been
conscious of it hour after hour, and felt that he
winced time and again when some of the callers
spoke even guardedly of the changes Barclay was
making in the old troop, changes all men except
the ultra-conservative ranker element (as the
ranker was so often constituted at that peculiar
time, be it understood) could see were for the
better.

"You and Barclay lead on, will you, Ned?"
said the major, in his genial way. "I wish to
speak with Mullane a moment." Whereat he
reined out to the right and waited for the big
Irishman to come lunging up. Mullane was already spurring close at his heels, gloomily eying
the combination in front. "There are Oirish and
Oirish," as one of their most appreciative and
broad-minded exponents, Private Terence Mulvaney, has told us; and it galled the veteran
dragoon to see his junior in rank bidden to ride
even for the moment at the head of the swiftly
moving column. So, reckless of the fact that his
individual spurt would call for a certain forcing
of the pace along his entire troop, now moving in
long column of twos, Mullane had spurred his

horse to close the twelve-yard gap between himself and the major's orderly, determined that there should be no conference of the powers in which he was not represented.

"Captain Mullane," said Brooks, "I see it is getting dusty. You might divide into sections, as 'D' troop has done, and keep fifty yards apart, so that the dust can blow aside and not choke your men."

"This is 'L' Troop, sorr, and my men are not babes in arrums," was Mullane's magnificent reply. At any other time he might have felt the pertinence of the suggestion, but here was a case where a doughboy captain, bedad, had instigated the measure for the comfort of his men. That was enough to damn it in the eyes of the old dragoon. The answer was shouted, too, with double intent. Mullane desired Barclay to hear what he thought of such over-solicitude; but Barclay, riding onward sturdily if not quite so easily as was Lawrence, gave no sign. He was listening, with head inclined, to the words of the keen campaigner on his right.

Brooks was quick to note the intention of the Irish officer, and equally quick to note the flushed and inflamed condition of his face, the thickness of his tongue. "So ho, my Celtic friend," thought he, as he saw that two canteens were swung on the off side of Mullane's saddle, one at the cantle under the rolled blanket, the other half shaded by the bulging folds of the overcoat at the pommel, "I suspected there was more whiskey than wit in your eagerness at the start; now I know it."

But even to Mullane the major would not speak discourteously. "We all know 'L' Troop is ready for anything, captain," he smilingly answered, "but I have to call for unusual exertion to-day, and the fresher they are to-night the better. Let them open out, as I say," he continued; and Mullane saw it was useless to put on further airs.

"You 'tind to it, sergeant," he grunted over his shoulder to his loyal henchman, and then, uninvited, ranged up alongside the leader.

The prairie was open here; the road split up into several tracks from time to time, and the men could have ridden platoon front without much difficulty for two or three miles. Away to the southeast the ground rose in slow, gradual, almost imperceptible slope to the edge of the far horizon, not a tree or shrub exceeding a yard in height breaking anywhere the dull monotony of the landscape. Eastward, miles and miles away, a line of low rolling hills framed the dull hues of the picture. Northward there was the same

almost limitless expanse of low, lazy undulation.
To the right front, the south and southwest, the
land seemed to fall away in even longer, lazier
billows, until it flattened out into a broad valley,
drained by some far-distant, invisible stream.
Only to the west and northwest, over their right
shoulders, was there gleam of something brighter.
The faint blue outline of the far-away Apache
range was still capped in places by glistening
white, while straight away to the northwest, back
of and beyond the dim dust-cloud through which
the swallow-tailed guidons were peeping, hovered
over their winding trail the bold and commanding
heights, Fort Worth's shelter against the keen
blasts that swept in winter-time across the prairie
from the upper valley of the Rio Bravo.   Four
hours out, and just where the road dipped into
that broad deep swale a quarter-mile behind the
rearmost troopers,—just where the wreck of one
of Fuller's wagons and the bones of two of Fuller's mules and the soft spongy mud to the west
of the trail told how the waters could gather there
in the rainy season and evaporate to nothingness
when needed in the dry,—a solitary stake driven
into the yielding soil bore on bullet-perforated
cross-board the legend, "20 miles to Worth and
only 20 rods to Hell."

Only twenty miles in four hours, with fresh

horses and the cool of the morning, and a paymaster with forty thousand dollars in deadly
danger some sixty to eighty miles away. Slow
going that, yet scientific. Not another drop of
water could those lively chargers hope to have
until they reached the springs at Crockett, forty
miles away. Thrice has Brooks halted for brief
ten minutes' rest, the resetting of saddles, etc.,
and now, after fifteen minutes' lively jog, he sig-
nals "walk" again, and glances back to watch the
march of his men. By this time the column is
long drawn out. The two troops are split up into
four sections each, riding a little over a dozen
men in a bunch; by this means they are relieved
from the ill effects of the choking clouds of dust.
Mullane halts with the major. It pleases him to
convey the impression to his men that Brooks
can't get along without him. A big pull at his
pommel canteen, ten minutes back, has temporarily braced him, and he wants to talk, whereas
Brooks, intent on the duty before him, wishes to
think.

"Hwat time will we make Crockett's, major?"

"Not before five or five-thirty," is the brief
answer.

"'L' Troop can do it in two hours less."

"So could 'D,' if it hadn't to push on again at
nightfall." Brooks answers in civil tone, despite

the hint conveyed by the brevity of his words,
despite the conviction that is growing on him as
he somewhat warily glances over his companion,
that what "L" might do its captain won't do if
he consults that canteen again.   Two silent but
keen-eared orderlies are sitting in saddle close beside their respective officers, and it will not do to
give his thoughts away.

Then Mullane tries another tack.   He seeks
confidential relations with his chief; and when
an Irishman has a man he is jealous of to talk
about and whiskey to start him, he needs no supply of facts; they bubble from his seething brain,
manufactured for the occasion.

"The Preacher was caught where he couldn't
get out of it," says he, with a leering wink at the
leading horseman.   "Is he larnin' his thrade from
Lawrence, afther robbin' him av his throop?"

And now Brooks fires up unexpectedly.   Turning quickly on the Irishman with anger in his
eyes, the major bends forward over the pommel.
"Captain Mullane," he says, so low that the near-
by troopers fail to catch his words, so distinctly
that the captain cannot fail to, "there are things
of more value in a trade than the tricks of it that
you seem to know so well.   You can learn more
from Captain Barclay that is worth knowing than
you can ever teach him, and I'll listen to no slur

at his expense. You've been drinking too much,
Mullane. Take my advice and pull the stopper
out of that canteen and put one on your tongue."

The Irishman boils up with wrath. The idea
of Major Mildmanners pitching into him—him,
that was once the pride of the Second Dragoons!
—and praising that white-livered parson! Whurroo! Mullane at the moment could have flung
commission and conscience to the wind, everything but that canteen. Nothing but the stern
and icy stare in Brooks's usually benignant eye
represses the outburst trembling on the tangling
tip of his tongue.

"If you knew—what I know, sorr, that man'd
not be ridin' wid his betthers," he begins, "and
it's this night that'll prove me wurrds."

CHAPTER XI.

It was at four o'clock of a blistering afternoon, twelve hours from the time of their start from the post, that the leaders in the long-extended column hove in sight of a patch of green down in a distant depression to the south that marked the site of Crockett Springs. Beyond it, hemming the broad, shallow valley, there rose a long wave of bare, desolate heights, rounded and billowing in soft and graceful contours as they rolled away northeastward, abrupt and jagged towards the south and southwest, where the stream seemed to have torn a pathway for the sudden torrents of the springtide that foamed away towards the broader valley of the Bravo. At the point where, rounding the nose of a low ridge, the trail twisted into view of Crockett's, the major halted to look back over his command, still tripping steadily onward in little bunches, each a dozen strong, each followed by its own little dust-cloud, each independent, apparently, of the others, yet moving as part of one harmonious train. Foremost, the group at the head of column had received accessions. Fuller, the sutler, finely

150

mounted and bristling with arms of the latest and
most approved pattern, backed by two sun-tanned
Texans from his ranch, had overtaken the command at noon, bent on sharing its fortunes in the
tussle anticipated with the outlaws; and they
were now riding with "head-quarters," from
which, on the other hand, two figures were missing,—Lawrence and one of the orderlies. As
early as two o'clock the ex-captain had pushed
on ahead, a double object in view, to warn
Cramer's troop of the coming of the Worth command and the tidings they bore of the Friday
gang, also to have a little party mount at once and
gallop northeast, ten miles to the Saba trail,—a
short cut from Worth to the San Saba Pass, used
by horsemen in the rainy season. Captain Cramer
might or might not have received warning of the
appearance of the gang in the valley below his
camp at the Springs; but the "Fridays," whoever
their leader, would certainly have friends and
confederates on the watch near Worth, friends
who would probably take that very short cut and
gallop at speed to warn the gang of the coming
vengeance. Oddly enough, it was not Brooks nor
Lawrence who was first to think of this, but Barclay. It was his modest suggestion at the noon
halt, a suggestion that was put in form of a question, that had opened the major's eyes. "I re-

member, sir," said he, "that the Springs lie in a sort of elbow; the trail runs nearly east and west for many miles beyond them, and nearly north and south on this side. Is there no way in which scouts could gallop across our left and give warning to those fellows?"

"By Jove!" said Brooks, "there's the old San Saba cut-off. What had we better do, Lawrence?" And Lawrence said, "Send at once a sergeant with a set of fours to the left, until they cut the trail, in order to prevent information going to the gang that way, and to report if any horsemen have already passed, which latter any old frontiersman can tell at a glance." Mullane, lurching drowsily in saddle all through the last stage, had thrown himself on the turf and gone sound asleep the moment the column halted. Only with extreme difficulty could he be aroused and made to understand what was wanted. Mr. Winn, standing silently by, turned his back on his temporary commander. He knew the Irish captain was well-nigh swamped with liquor, and he had no wish to bear witness against him. Those were days so close to the war that officers, old and new, still thought more of what a man had done than of what he was doing, and Mullane had been a gallant trooper. "You 'tind to it, sergeant," was again the Irishman's com-

prehensive order to his first sergeant when at last
he grasped the significance of Brooks's words, and
five horsemen rode away at the lope to the left
front the moment the column again mounted.
Again did Brooks see fit to caution his leading
troop commander. "I am afraid you have sam-
pled that whiskey once too often, Mullane. No
more of it now, or you'll go to pieces when you
are most needed," he muttered, then rode on to
the head of column.

And the prediction came true. At the very
next halt Mullane had fallen into a stupor so
heavy that it was found impossible to rouse him.
The assistant surgeon with the column made brief
examination, then unslung and removed the canteen at the captain's pommel, and whispered his
conclusion,—"Better leave his horse and orderly
here with him."

"Then," said the major, briefly, "Winn, you
command 'L' Troop." And when again the column mounted, Barclay rode back and directed his
leading section to incline to the right, so that they
passed the lonely little group, the two horses
placidly cropping at the scant herbage, the orderly squatting with averted face, filled at once
with shame and sympathy, the recumbent figure
sprawled upon the prairie, its bloated red visage
buried in the blue-sleeved arms. Barclay's rear-

ward sections instinctively followed the lead, and
only furtive glances were cast, and no audible
comments made. The ranks were full of tough
characters in those days, yet imbued with a
strange fidelity in certain lines that reminds one
of the dog immortalized by Bret Harte at Red
Gulch,—the dog that had such deep sympathy for
a helplessly drunken man. There was nothing in
their code to prevent their stealing from Uncle
Sam, their captain, or any other victim, but to
hint that an officer or a friend was drunk would
have been the height of impropriety.

Winn, not Mullane, therefore, led "The
Devil's Own," as Mullane's troop—together with
others, no doubt—had been appropriately designated. Barclay followed at the head of "D."
When nearing Crockett Springs at five o'clock, a
dim speck of courier came twisting out upon the
trail to meet them, and Brooks long after recalled
the thought that came to him as he read the de-
spatch that reached him there. It was from Lawrence:

"Cramer got wind of the gang early this morning, followed with thirty men into the San Saba,
had sharp fight, lost three men and many horses,
and is corralled out there, about fifteen miles
southeast. Cramer himself wounded, Dr. Augus-

tin killed. Courier says most of Friday gang gone to San Saba Pass. You, of course, must push on to save Pennywise and his money. I take five men and horses here and hasten to pull Cramer out of the hole. Think you now justified in attacking gang wherever found. No doubt who were Cramer's assailants. Expect to reach him before six and have one more square fight out of Texas. Hastily,

" L."

"By heaven," cried Brooks, as he turned to Fuller and the little party riding with him, all studying his face with anxious eyes, "it's lucky we got here with our horses in good shape. Cramer is in a scrape somewhere out in the Range. Lawrence has gone to his aid, and there'll only be time for a bite at Crockett's; then we must push on and go ahead to the Pass." Then, dropping into thought, "Now, which of Laura Waite's victims will most welcome a square fight,—the man she wronged by dropping, or the man she wronged by taking?"

Two hours later, refreshed by cooling draughts from the brook that bubbled away from the Springs, their nostrils sponged out, their saddles reset, their stomachs gladdened by a light feed, the horses of the two troops seemed fit for a

chase, despite their sixty-mile march since dawn.
A courier, galloping ahead, had borne Brooks's
directions that coffee should be ready for his men,
and Cramer's camp guard had found time to add
substantials to that comforting fluid. Only half
an hour did the major delay, but even in that
time the horses had a quick rub-down with wisps
of hay, and the men themselves swung into saddle with an air that seemed to say, "There's fun
ahead!" The sun was shining aslant from low
down in the western sky as the column once more
jogged away on the dusty trail, Barclay's troop
now in the lead, opening out just as it had
marched most of the day, while Winn, between
whom and the new captain there had passed a few
courteous yet rather formal words at one or two
of the halts, gave to Mullane's old first sergeant
the charge of the leading section, and himself
rode at the distant rear of column, for by dusk,
if at all, straggling would be likely, and straggling would have to be suppressed with a firm
hand. The sun was at their backs now: away to
the front lay the rift in the hills through which
wound the San Saba road, and off to the right
front, well to the southeast, somewhere among
those jagged bluffs just beginning to tinge with
gold about their sharp and saw-like crests, lay the
scene of Cramer's morning tussle with the out-

laws, who, as all now realized, must have opened
on him from ambush and shot down several horses
and not a few men before the troopers could reply. No further news had come from him, however. The courier who brought the first news
said he had to run the gauntlet, although only a
few of the gang seemed to be hanging about the
scene of the fight,—their main body, as he had
previously reported, having gone in the direction
of the Pass. Brooks well knew that the moment
he reached the foot-hills he would have to move
with caution, throwing out advanced guards and,
where possible, flankers. He knew that he would
need every man, and believed that Cramer's people, now that Lawrence had gone to join them,
could take care of themselves; but the courier's
story, told to eager ears, had "told" in more ways
than one. His description of the ambuscade, the
way Cramer, the doctor, Sergeant O'Brien, and
others at the head of column were tumbled at the
first fire, all had tended to make the head of
Brooks's column an unpopular place to ride,—at
least less popular than earlier in the day. Fuller
and his men decided that their horses would be
the better for an hour or two of rest at the cantonment, and so the column moved on without
them.

Longer grew the shadows and loftier the range

far to the front, as once more the pace quickened
to the trot, and Brooks and his men jogged on.
The doctor, a gifted young practitioner whom
Collabone held in high regard, seemed still to
think that he should have been allowed to take
an orderly and his instruments and gallop out on
Lawrence's trail to the aid of Cramer's wounded.
"Then what is to become of mine?" asked the
major, calmly. "I'm sorry for Cramer, sorry his
doctor is killed, but we may need you any moment
more than he does. No, Lawrence has gone to
him; he'll do what he can to make the wounded
comfortable, leave a small guard with them, and
then guide the rest of Cramer's troop through the
range to the San Saba, join either Pennywise's
party or ours, and between us we ought to give
those fellows a thrashing they'll never forget,—
if only they'll stand and take it,—if only," he
added below his breath, "they don't lay for us in
some of those deep twisting cañons where twenty
men could overthrow a thousand."

The doctor admitted the force of his superior's
argument, and said no word. All the same, however, his eyes kept wandering off from time to
time towards the foot-hills at the southeast, now
turning to violet in shade, "like half-mourning,"
said the doctor to Galahad, as, only half content,
he dropped back to ride a few moments at the

latter's side. "And it won't be long," he added to himself, "before they'll be shrouded in deep black. Pray God there's no ill omen in that!"

And now the road began to rise, very slowly, very gently as yet, but perceptibly, towards the still distant range. The long, spindle-shanked shadows of the horses had disappeared. The sun, yellow-red, was just sinking below the horizon through the dust-clouds in their wake, when one of the foremost troopers, close at Barclay's heels, muttered, "It's somethin' movin', anyhow, and what is it if it ain't a horse?" And Barclay and the doctor, turning in saddle, caught his eye. "I seen it a minute ago away out yonder towards them buttes," continued the soldier, pointing out across the prairie to their right front, "and I couldn't be sure then. It's comin' this way, whatever it is, comin' fast. Look, sir! There it is again!"

And with all their eyes Barclay and the doctor gazed, but could see no moving object. Only the rolling prairie, growing darker, dimmer every minute, only the sun-tipped ridge and buttes and shining pinnacles far away towards the San Saba. And still the relentless trot went on, and the major's head was never turned; yet his orderly, too, was ducking and peering from time to time off to the southeast, just where the trooper had

pointed. Barclay, cautioning his sergeant to keep
a steady trot, spurred forward, the doctor following.

"What do you see?" they asked, and the orderly too stretched forth a grimy gauntlet.

"Thought I saw a horse, sir. Some of 'K'
Troop's, maybe, for there was no rider."

With this corroborative evidence, Barclay
hailed the major. "Major, may I send a man or
two out in that direction?" he asked. "Two of
our people report seeing a horse galloping this
way."

But, even as he spoke, over a distant divide,
popping up against the sky just long enough to
catch the eyes of half a dozen men at once, a
black dot darted into view and then came bounding down the long, gradual incline, looming
larger and larger as it ran; presently the body
and legs could be made out, and then the sweeping mane and tail,—a riderless horse, a cavalry
horse probably, coming at eager speed to join his
comrade creatures in the long column. Cavalry
horse undoubtedly, as, bounding nearer and
nearer, the flapping rein, the dangling, black-
hooded stirrups, the coarse gray blanket, and the
well-known saddle could be distinguished, a grue-
some sight to trooper eyes, harbinger of disaster
if not of death in almost every case,—a cavalry

charger riderless! And at last, as with piteous neigh the laboring steed came galloping straightway on, a cry went up from two or three soldier throats at the instant, a wail of soldier sorrow: "God save us, fellows! it's Blarney—it's the colonel's own!" Officers and men, they swarmed about the weary, panting, trembling creature, as hope died in every heart at what they saw: the saddle and blanket, the old overcoat, rolled at the pommel, that so often had stood between Ned Lawrence and the Texas gales, were all dripping with blood, yet Blarney had never a scratch.

11

CHAPTER XII.

THE moon was throwing black shadows into the deep cleft in the San Saba, where the Crockett trail twisted along beside the swift-running rivulet, that rose in the heart of the hills and bubbled merrily away until lost in the westward valley and the brook that found its source at the springs far out under the foot-hills towards the Bravo. Slowly, wearily, warily, half a dozen troopers on jaded horses were feeling their way up the pass, a veteran corporal full thirty yards ahead of his fellows leading on. With the advance rode an officer whose shoulder-straps, gleaming on the shell jacket sometimes worn in the mounted service immediately after the war, seemed almost too bright and new to accord with the dust-grimed chevrons and trimmings of his comrades. New and brilliant, too, were the hilt and scabbard of the sabre that dangled by his side. New and "green" the men of his command had believed him to be, in cavalry matters at least, when first he joined them some weeks before, but the most casehardened old customer among their seasoned troopers had abandoned that view before

162

ever they started on this scout after a gang of
notorious outlaws, and now a new and very different theory was grinding its way into their tired
brains,—that the "Doughboy Dragoon," as they
had earlier dubbed him, "Captain Gallyhad," as
one of them heard he was called, could give them
points in covering the front of a column that were
worth knowing, even if they had been learned in
a doughboy regiment and among the Sioux. It
would be a smart "Friday" that managed to ambuscade old Brooks's column that cloudless, moon-
lit, breezeless night, for, with that veteran's full
consent, as well as to his infinite relief, Captain
Barclay had himself gone forward with the advance the moment they began to wind in among
the hills, and there at the post of danger he had
held his way, alert and vigilant, despite long hours
in saddle that had told heavily on more than half
the command, calm and brave despite the fact
that their welcome to the westward portal of the
Pass was the sight of poor Blarney running to
them for shelter, sympathy, and companionship,
covered with the blood of his beloved rider.

And what was that rider's fate? It was now
almost eleven o'clock, and no man knew. Only
briefly had they halted and flocked about the
panting steed, for stern was the need that held
them to their course. With awe-stricken faces

and compressed lips they looked into each other's
eyes, as though to ask, What next? Who next?
The major, tender-hearted as a woman, well-nigh
choked with distress and anxiety as he turned to
Barclay for counsel; and long before the rearmost of the column had reached the spot the decision had been made. The leaders were again
pushing on. Young Brayton, with half a dozen
troopers, had been despatched southwestward
along the *falda*, ordered to search high and low
for Lawrence, dead or alive. There was only
one theory,—that, pushing eagerly ahead to the
relief of Cramer's crippled troop, the gallant ex-
captain had taken no thought of personal danger;
the old instinct of leadership had possessed him,
and, foremost of his little squad, he had been
picked off by lurking bushwackers of the outlaws,
crouching like Indians in the shelter of the rocks,
and had fallen another victim of their desperado
efforts. "One more fight in Texas," indeed.
Poor, brave, warm-hearted Ned! That one more
fight, reported in Washington by an indulgent
department commander, might bring about im-
mediate measures for his restoration to the army;
but was it worth the risk? Was it worth what
might befall those motherless children, praying
for father hour after hour that livelong day?
Should it have been permitted, had there been

any one to prevent, in view of the fact that no longer was there soldier duty to lead him on? The government had released him from all that, had bidden him go. It had no further use for the services of such as he; it had turned him loose upon the world, with heavy stoppages against the stipulated *bonus*. "Oh, what right had he," cried Brooks, "to forget those babies back at Worth, well knowing as he must that no man's life is worth a hair in front of the rifles of that outlaw gang, much less an enemy such as Lawrence has shown himself to be?" The major's heart and head were heavy as once more the order forward was given. With every inclination to turn from his course with his entire command, to hasten in search of Lawrence's little party and Cramer's halted men, he well knew that should the paymaster and his precious thousands fall into the outlaw hands of the Friday gang he would be held responsible, even though San Saba's cantonment sent with him a force of forty men.

Once within the jaws of the Pass, the little detachment had closed on the head of column, the advance guard, Barclay's leading section, riding on and dispersing itself under his instructions, while Brooks held the other sections until Winn's men were all closed up, bringing with them the little squads that had scouted towards the short

cut of the San Saba and had found no living
soul in sight, yet had followed fresh hoof-tracks
coming their way for miles. Whoever they were,
the scouts of the gang were well ahead; whoever
he was, "Friday" by this time knew the troops
were coming. Then, with the flankers scouring
the slopes well out to right and left wherever
possible, Brooks's main body too had entered the
winding defile and was lost in the bowels of the
earth.

At eleven o'clock a watcher, gazing back into
the broad shallow depression in which lay Crockett's, and then northward to the low-lying hills
along the trail to Worth, could have seen no
gleam of light far or near that would speak of
human habitation or life or movement, no sign,
in fact, of life of any kind; yet no sooner was the
last shadowy form of horse and trooper swallowed
up in the black gloom of the defile, no sooner had
the last faint click of iron-shod hoofs died away
in the hidden distance, than there slowly rose
from behind the shelter of a clump of rocks, far
out to the right of the trail, a crouching figure
that went almost on all-fours to the edge of the
rivulet, slunk away down the bank, dodging
swiftly, softly, from boulder to boulder, until it
disappeared around a little shoulder of bluff five
hundred yards away, was lost to view a moment,

then reissued into the moonlight, this time in saddle, swinging, cowboy fashion, a *riata* about its head as it rode. Spinning up the slopes and out of the stream-bed, away it went, careering up the billowy rise to the south, and was presently lost to view a second time behind some castellated rocks along the crest. Three minutes more, and these began to glow along their eastward face with the light of some unseen fire that flared for perhaps a minute somewhere about the hidden base of the group, and then, far away to the southeast, far out among the buttes and knolls in the heart of the range, there was a sudden flash of brilliant light, just as though some one had touched off in front of a reflector a pound or so of rifle powder. The hills for one second were lighted up, then as suddenly relapsed into gloom. The blaze at the ledge so close at hand was promptly doused, and the night rolled on, calm, placid, and unbroken.

When the first streak of dawn crept into the orient sky, Barclay's shadowy scouts were issuing from the San Saba on the farther side and halting for the coming of the main body. Neither those who led the advance nor those out on either flank, where flankers were at all possible, had seen a sign of outlaw, cowboy, even of human being, outside their own array. Not only had the Friday gang vanished from the neighborhood of the

Pass, but, what was most mysterious, not a sign
had appeared of paymaster or escort, who were
due at Crockett's early this very morning.
Brooks, picking out the lightest rider in his weary
column, sent him on the liveliest horse to warn
Pennywise and his escort, provided he could find
him at the San Saba camp, of what had taken
place, notify him that they would here await his
coming, and meantime ordered dismount, unsad-
dle, and graze, and in two minutes every charger
was divested of his load, and many of them were
kicking and rolling on the turf.

Twenty-four hours had the command been in
saddle, except for the required halts and a long
two hours during the dead of night, when leading
their wearied steeds or crouching beside them at
rest, while Barclay and his scouts explored the
overhanging heights and listened eagerly for
sound of coming troopers from the eastward. But
for the waning moon there would have been hours
of total darkness. Ninety miles, all told, had
they travelled, and now, wearied though they
were, nine out of ten of the men were chafing
with wrath that the wily gang had managed to
escape them. Whither were they gone, and
where on earth was the paymaster, were the questions. Certainly not through the Pass, for there
were no fresh hoof-prints. Could it be that,

balked in their plan to overwhelm the escort by
this coming of at least an equal force, the gang
had turned back angered and thrown themselves
on Cramer's crippled party with the view of getting away with the horses, arms, and equipments?
Certainly none of Cramer's people had made their
way by the game trails over the range to join
them, but there was reason for that: Lawrence
had never succeeded in reaching Cramer.

Sad, wearied, and depressed, Major Brooks
seated himself on a saddle-blanket to take counsel
with his officers, now reduced to three,—Barclay,
Winn, and the doctor. He missed Mullane,
stanch old fighter that he was, for Mullane knew
most of the country thoroughly, and had been
posted for months at the Rio San Saba, now only
some twenty miles to the east. He sorely missed
Lawrence, for on him he had often leaned. He
was beginning to take vast comfort in Barclay, to
be sure, but now Barclay, Winn, the doctor, men
and horses, the entire command, in fact, had
come to a stand-still. There was no use in going
farther east; there the country was comparatively
open and rolling, and the gang would hardly dare
attack forty troopers on the wide prairie. Besides, the nearest water in that direction was
twenty miles away; the little rivulet rising in the
heart of the hills was ten miles behind them, and

already horses were thirsting and men emptying
their canteens. Blankly the major stared up into
Barclay's drawn and almost haggard face. "Can
you think of anything we ought to do?" he asked,
and, in asking, Brooks was a far better soldier
than the man who, having exhausted his own re-
sources, thought it *infra dig.* to invite suggestions
from his juniors.

"Just one, sir. Sergeant McHugh tells me he
once came out here hunting with Captain Mullane, and that they took a light spring wagon
right over the range southeast of Crockett's, the
way Cramer went. It is a much longer way
round, but a more open way. The trail must lie
some eight or ten miles off here to the south, or
west of south. Could it be that the gang only
started from the place of Cramer's ambuscade as
though to go to the Pass and then veered around
again and covered that trail, and for some reason
have been expecting the paymaster that way after
all?"

Worn and weary as he was, Brooks staggered
to his feet at once, his face going paler still. "By
heaven, Barclay, if that's possible, they've had
uninterrupted hours in which to deal with Pennywise already! It is possible," he added, with
misery in the emphasis of his tone. "I remember
having heard of that trail, but never thought it

practicable for an ambulance. Then there is work before us yet. Call Sergeant McHugh," he cried. The word was passed among the wearied groups, where, squatting or lying, the men had thrown themselves upon the ground, and presently, rubbing his red eyes, a stocky little Irish sergeant came trudging up to his commander and silently touched the visor of his worn old cap.

"Can you guide us by the shortest route from here to the trail you spoke of to Captain Barclay?" asked the major.

Mac turned and gazed away southwestward along the line of the San Saba hills.

"I don't think we could miss it, sir, if we followed the foot-hills."

"Then we must try it," said Brooks, decidedly, half turning to the silent officers as he spoke. "Let the horses graze ten minutes more and get all the dew and grass they can, then we'll push for it."

And so, just before five, hungry, weary, and weak,—some of the men at least,—the little squadron clambered into saddle and once more moved away. No need to leave any one to say which way they'd gone; the trail showed all that. Silently they headed for the broad valley of the Bravo, miles away to the invisible west. Once across a little rise in the *falda*, Brooks struck the slow trot he had learned long years before from the beloved major of his old regiment, and doggedly the column took it up and followed. Not a mile had they gone when the sun came peering up over the heights far in their wake; for a few minutes the dew flashed and sparkled on the turf before it died beneath that fiery breath, and still no man spoke. Sound sleep by night, a cold plunge at dawn, and the hot tin of soldier coffee send the morning tongues of a column *en route* "wagging like sheep's tails," say the troopers, but it takes a forced all-night march, following an all-day ride, followed by a morning start without either cold plunge or hot coffee, to stamp a column with the silence of a Quaker meeting. Let no man think, however, the fight is out of its heart, unless he is suffering for a scrimmage on any terms. Men wake up with a snap at sound of the first shot; dull eyes flash in answer to the bugle challenge, and worn and wearied troopers "take a brace" that means mischief to the foe at the first note that tells of trouble ahead. Just two miles out there came the test to Brooks's men, and there was none so poor as to be found wanting.

Two miles out, and the column woke up at the cry, "Yon comes a courier!" and coming he was, "hell to split," said Sergeant McHugh, from afar off over the rolling prairie to the southwest. Five

minutes brought him within hail,—a corporal
from the camp on the Rio San Saba, on foaming
horse, who came tugging at both reins, sputtering
and plunging, up to the head of column, and
blurted out his news. "I thought you was the
escort, sir,—the paymaster's escort. They left
camp at nine last night, and at two this morning
Corporal Murphy got back, shot, and said they
were corralled in the hills on the old trail. The
captain is coming along with twenty men, and
sent me ahead. They must be ten miles from
here yet, sir."

"The paymaster, or the captain?" asked
Brooks, his heart beating hard, but his face imperturbable.

"Both, sir, I reckon; one one way and the
other the other."

Then Brooks signalled over his shoulder.
"We've got to gallop, Barclay. It's neck or
nothing now." And some horses even then were
drooping at the trot.

Six o'clock now. Six miles from the eastward
mouth of the Pass, and spurs were plying here
and there throughout the column, for many found
their horses lagging sorely. Barclay on his
splendid blooded bay was far out to the front, the
corporal courier with him, for theirs were the
only mounts that could stand another forcing of

the pace. Rearward, three or four horses, exhausted, were being gathered up by a burly sergeant, and with their weary riders led slowly along the trail. Six-fifteen:—Barclay and his corporal were but dots along the *falda* now, and moving swiftly. Then at a higher point, in plain view, one dot began circling to the left at speed. Every man knew what that meant, and the signal was answered by another spurt. The sun was telling at last. The dew had dried, but along the turf there was but little dust to rise, and Brooks could keep most of his men together. Far off to the left, all eyes could see now the sign that told that rival rescuers were gaining. The little squad from the San Saba camp came spurring along the beaten trail, betrayed by the cloud of dust that rose above them. Young Connolly, the guidon-bearer of Barclay's troop, unfurled his color and set it flapping in the rising breeze in trooper challenge; and down the column set and haggard faces lighted up with the gleam of soldier joy. It was to be a race,—a race to the rescue. Six-thirty, and over a low ridge went Brooks and Winn, close followed by their orderlies; far away, midway up the opposite slope, stretched a slender, twisting, traversing seam,—the winding trail to Crockett's. The black dots in the lead were now three in number, darting towards two others,

black dots, too, some four miles away and to the
right front, right in among the hills. "Keep it
up, lads! the quicker to water and rest!" are the
major's words now, and spurs set home again,
despite equine grunts in protest. Six-forty, and
the dots in front are blacker and bigger and popping about, three of them, at least, in lively motion, checking suddenly, then darting to and fro,
and the cry bursts from the leader's lips, "By
God, they're at it! Now, lads, for all you're
worth, come on!" Six-forty-five, and, rounding
a projecting spur, a shoulder from the range,
Brooks, Winn, and the doctor burst in view of a
scene that banishes the last thought of weariness.
Barely a mile or so away, a rocky ledge lies beyond and parallel with the trail. Its jagged crest
is spitting smoke and fire. Its smoother slopes,
towards the east, are dotted in places by the bodies
of dead or dying horses, and in places, too, by
other, smaller forms, apparently stiff and motion-
less. Off the trail, as though dragged there by
affrighted and agonized animals, lies an overturned ambulance, its six draught-mules out-
stretched upon the turf about it; so, too, are other
quadrupeds, troop-horses evidently. Well back
of the ruined wagon, some trusty soul has rallied
the remaining troop-horses, while most of their
riders, sprawled upon the turf or behind impro-

vised rifle-pits, stick manfully to their duty.
"Friday's" ambuscade, in the still hours of the
night, has cost the government heavily in horses,
men, and mules, but old Pennywise's precious
safe is guarded still, and every rush the outlaws
make to get it is met by relentless fire. Six-fifty,
and, leaving on the field six outlawed forms that
will never fight again, the baffled relics of the
Fridays are scurrying away into the fastnesses of
the range before the labored rush and sputtering
fire of Brooks's men, and Galahad, with his corporal comrade, far in the lead, gets the last compliments of the departing gang. Another gallant
horse goes down, and Galahad's for the time goes
free, his rider falling fainting from exhaustion
and loss of blood.

CHAPTER XIII.

OLD Frazier's face was sad to see when, two days later, all the harrowing details of that night's work were received at Worth. Hours before, in answer to courier from Crockett's, Dr. Collabone, with steward, attendants, and such ambulances as there were, had been put *en route* for the Springs. Two other troops had been hurried to the field, and Mrs. Blythe, with streaming eyes, was straining to her heart two motherless children, now orphaned by that "one more square fight in Texas." Gallant Ned Lawrence! Far on the way to Cramer's bewildered force they found his body, shot from ambush through and through in two places. Yet, said his weeping orderly, he had clung to the saddle nearly a mile. Oh, the wrath at Department Head-Quarters and along the line of posts and camps against that gang, made up, as so many knew it must be made, mainly of the thugs and deserters offscoured from the army in days when moral character as vouched for was no requisite before enlistment! Among the dead upon the field was found the body of a once trusted sergeant of Lawrence's troop; but the other outlaws were Mexicans or jailbirds, strange to the soldiers who turned them curiously over. Pennywise, scared half to death and dreadfully shaken by the capsizing of his wagon, was otherwise unscathed; his clerk was shot, his driver sorely wounded; two of the San Saba escort were killed, and others hit. Brooks, with Captain Haines from the San Saba, pushed on until at noon he reached Cramer's people, now reinforced by Fuller and his men and by the shame-stricken Mullane. By nightfall his exhausted horses were drinking their fill from the stream. The two wounded officers, Barclay and Cramer, with half a dozen troopers, were being made as comfortable as possible.

By dawn of the next day Mullane's pleading had overpowered Brooks, whose heart was wrung at the contemplation of such unrequited losses, and, taking Lieutenant Winn and forty troopers with him, the Irish captain, given a chance as he prayed to redeem himself, marched away westward from the cantonment at Crockett's, bent on overtaking the outlaws in the Apache mountains, whither they had gone, burdened by half a dozen wounded, so said the one prisoner, who, unable to bear the torment of jolting along on horseback with an arm bullet-smashed at the elbow, had begged to be left behind. He was a mere boy, whose elder brother had been for years a fugitive from justice and of late a prominent member of the gang, and it was by the side of that mortally wounded ruffian they found the youngster weeping, more from grief than from pain, only a mile away from the scene of the second ambuscade.

Verily the men who planned those death-traps were masters of their villanous trade! "Concentrate all your first shots on the officers," were the instructions; "get them down, and the men will be helpless as sheep." Cramer, his doctor, and his first sergeant had fallen at the first fire, and that little command was paralyzed. Vigilant bushwackers, schooled for years in Indian fighting, watching the Crockett trail against the coming of other leaders, had easily recognized Lawrence as he rode galloping on at the head of his half-dozen, and the "one more square fight" proved but a one-sided affair after all. Poor Ned knew he had his death-wounds at the instant, yet whipped out his revolver and ordered, "Charge!" and charge they did upon the scattering, cowardly crew that fled before them on their fresh horses until the trooper leader tumbled from his saddle, dead without a groan; and then, at safe distance, his assassins turned and jeered their helpless pursuers. How the veterans of "D" Troop clustered about their old-time captain's lifeless form that

night, and, weary though they were after forty
hours of sleepless chase and scout and battle, implored the major to let them start at once upon
the outlaws' trail! The same tactics that had
halted Cramer's men and murdered Lawrence had
been played on the escort from San Saba. Rid-
dling the ambulance at the first volley, yet in the
dim moonlight missing the lieutenant commanding, who happened to be riding at the moment on
the flank of his column instead of at the head, the
sudden volley felled a sergeant, but left the subaltern full of fight, and he rallied his temporarily
stampeded troopers not four hundred yards away,
and charged back on the Fridays with a splendid
dash that drove them helter-skelter to the rocks.
Then, dismounting, he had stood them off superbly until rescue came.

Not for another forty-eight hours could old
Pennywise be induced to go on to Worth.
Though there was reassurance in the fact that the
Fridays were scattered over far Western Texas by
that time (some never stopping, as it turned out,
until safe from pursuit beyond the Bravo), the
veteran money-changer's nerve was sorely shaken.
He had not half the pluck of his punctured clerk,
who, though shot by a Henry rifle bullet through
the left arm and across the breast outside the ribs,
declared himself fit to take even a hot and feverish

drive and go with the payment. Fuller and his ranchmen stuck manfully to that much desired safe, and announced their intention of protecting the paymaster at all hazards. The wounds of Cramer and Barclay had been most skilfully treated by the young doctor before Collabone reached them; thanks to the perfect habits and vigorous constitution of the latter, there was nothing to prevent his transportation by easy stages back to Worth at the end of the week, and thither he seemed strangely eager to go. Thither they had borne the remains of poor Lawrence, and there with all military honors had they buried all that was mortal of the loved yet luckless comrade. There, her own heart sorely wrung, Mrs. Blythe was doing her utmost to comfort weeping Ada, whose burly little brother was fortunately too young to feel the desolation of their position. But, flat on his back, Barclay had pencilled to the loving-hearted woman a little note that bore her a world of comfort, despite the suffering imposed by a mandate to reveal its contents to no one but her husband; for when a woman has news—good news, great news—to tell, a husband falls far short of the demands of the situation.

Barclay's wound had been dangerous at the time, mainly because the bullet had grazed an artery below the knee and brought on profuse

bleeding that, unnoticed in the excitement of the
running fight, sapped him of his strength and
left him swooning; but Collabone and his assistant declared it healing perfectly and that not even
a limp would remain to betray ¯it.   One week
from the day of the spirited skirmish in which he
had played so prominent and gallant a part, Sir
Galahad was lifted into the ambulance and started
for Worth at the very moment the general commanding the department was forwarding to Washington his report of the affair, urgently recom-
mending the bestowal of a brevet upon the new
captain of "D" Troop and a pension upon the
children of his whole-souled, hapless predecessor;
but, coupling his recommendations with ill-con-
sidered yet natural reference to the injustice with
which Captain and Brevet Lieutenant-Colonel
Lawrence had been treated, he succeeded only in
entombing the paper in some private pigeon-hole,
whence it was resurrected long months after, too
late to be of use.

After the manner of the army, the garrison at
Worth had ceased all outward sign of mourning
by the time Barclay reached the post, and almost
everybody was ready to devote himself or herself to the amelioration of his condition.   Mrs.
Frazier, with a motherly eye to business, had
lost no time in urging upon her liege the pro-

priety—indeed, the imperative necessity—of his riding out to meet the wounded officer and moving him at once under the shelter of their roof. Amanda could and should give up her room (she was only too glad to), and the girls could sleep together; then the mother and daughters would have sole charge of the nursing of this most eligible young man. What might not be accomplished by such a matron and such dear girls under such exceptional circumstances? Indeed, Frazier was given to understand that he must do it, for if Barclay was allowed to return to his own quarters right next door to the Winns'—and Mr. Winn away—who could say what couldn't be said?—what wouldn't be said? "Everybody knew that Laura Winn had been doing her best," said Mrs. Frazier, "to reset her nets and lure her whilom lover within the meshes," and this would give her opportunities immeasurable. Frazier had a sleepless night of it. He could not combat his wife's theories, though he would not admit the truth of all she asserted. "But," said he, "everybody will see through the scheme at a glance."

"I don't care if they do. I don't care what they say," said his energetic and strategic spouse. "The end justifies the means. Something must be done for the girls you've buried out here in this wilderness. As for Laura Winn, better a sneer at my precautions than a scandal for lack of them."

But Frazier remonstrated: "Barclay isn't the man to get mixed up in a scandal," said he.

"But Laura Winn wouldn't flinch at it," said she, "and it's the way the woman acts—not the man—that sets people talking;" wherein was Mrs. Frazier schooled beyond the sphere in which she moved. At her bidding, Frazier sent for young Brayton, who had marched back with the detachment not sent in chase, told him of Mrs. Frazier's benevolent plans for his captain's comfort, and suggested that such of Barclay's things as he might need be sent over beforehand,—"so as to have everything ready, you know."

The youngster looked embarrassed, said he would attend to it, but immediately sought Major Brooks, who was doing a good deal of resting at the time. "What am I to say to Colonel Frazier, sir?" he asked. "The colonel tells me Mrs. Frazier has a room all ready for Captain Barclay and wishes me to send over a lot of things, and I have a message from the captain saying he will probably arrive day after to-morrow and to have his room ready; and, he adds, in case any one plans to put him elsewhere, to decline in his name."

"Oh, wise young judge!" growled Brooks to

himself. Every day was adding to his respect for Galahad.

"I can't decline the commanding officer's invitation, can I, sir?" asked Brayton, in conclusion.

"No, you can't with safety," said the major, "but I'll speak to Collabone—— No," he added, abruptly, as he reflected that Mrs. Frazier might eventually hear of it, Collabone being a man who knew no guile and told everybody anything he knew. "No. You tell Collabone what the captain wishes, and let him fix it." And so between the three it was arranged, through the couriers at that time going back and forth every day, that Barclay should be notified of the honor in store for him. And notified he was, and gravely passed the letter over to Æsculapius Junior.

"Help me out of this, doctor, in some way," he said. "I wish to be nobody's guest." And so, when old Frazier did actually mount a horse and, with Amanda in a stylish habit beaming at his side, did actually ride forth—the first time he'd been in saddle in a year—and meet Barclay's ambulance full a thousand yards out from the post, and bade him thrice welcome to the room they had prepared for him, Barclay beamed back his thanks and appreciations, and bade the colonel believe he would never forget his kindness and Mrs. Frazier's, but that he had every possible com-

fort awaiting him at his own quarters, and could
never consent to incommoding Mrs. Frazier or
the young ladies. Indeed, the doctor had made
other and very different plans for him,—as indeed the doctor had. And Frazier rode back
vaguely relieved, yet crestfallen. He knew Barclay and the doctor were right. He knew he
himself shrank from such throwing of his daughters at a fellow's head; and then he quailed at the
thought of Mrs. Frazier's upbraidings, for she,
honest woman, felt it a mother's duty to provide
for her precious lambs, the more so because their
father was so culpably indifferent, if not shame-
fully negligent.

A balked and angered woman was Mrs. Frazier
at the captain's politely veiled refusal to come and
be nursed and captured under her roof. Tartaric
acid tinged the smiles of her innocent children
the next few days, and if ever there was a time
when it behooved Laura Winn to be on her guard
and behave with the utmost reserve as regarded
her next-door neighbor, it was here and now. She
could have read the danger signal in the Fraziers'
greeting at parade that very evening, as, most be-
comingly attired, she strolled languidly down the
line at the side of Æsculapius Junior, who, after
seeing his patient comfortably stowed in bed,
came forth to find her on the piazza, full of sym-

pathetic interest and eager to know what she
could do or make or have made in the way of ap-
petizing dainties for the sufferer. Nor did she
let him free until he found refuge in the midst
of the deeply interested group in front of the
colonel's quarters.

This was Tuesday evening, and only Brooks,
Blythe, and Brayton were permitted to intrude
upon the invalid after the long hours' trundle
over the prairie roads. On the morrow the paymaster was to take his ambulance, escort, and
emptied safe on the back track to Crockett's, and
Barclay was to be allowed to see Mrs. Blythe;
but, for the night, rest and quiet were enjoined.
In answer to his queries, he was told that the
latest news reported Mullane, Winn, and Bralligan scouring the Apache range, while Captain
Haight, with forty men, was patrolling towards
the Bravo. The post was flush with money. Fuller's bar was doing a rousing business, and Lieutenant Trott, guarding the stores turned over by
Winn, was wondering when and in what shape
the money value of the stores not turned over was
to be paid to him, for the time was past, Winn
was far, far away, no package of money had come
for him, and Mrs. Winn calmly said it was no
affair of hers and she had no knowledge when or
by what hand it would be forthcoming. It was

conceded at Worth that, in view of the danger in
which her husband stood, both afield and at home,
more anxiety and less adornment would better
have become the lady, as she outshone all other
women present when the line of infantry officers
broke ranks at dismissal of parade.

CHAPTER XIV.

A WEEK rolled by, a week little Jim Lawrence and other small boys long remembered for the good things they had to eat and drink; and now Galahad was sitting up again at his quarters, doing very well, said both doctors, so well that he could be out on the shaded piazza in a reclining chair, said Brayton,—but wouldn't, said Blythe, —and for good reasons, said the Fraziers feminine, "because then there'd be no dodging Laura Winn, if, indeed, he has succeeded thus far." True, he had not ventured outside his doors, and no one had seen her venture within them. True, Mrs. Frazier, Mrs. Blythe, and other motherly women had been to visit him,—Mrs. Frazier frequently,—and Mrs. Winn had been most particular in her daily inquiries,—"most persistent," said the Frazier girls. Those were days in which milk was a luxury in far-away Texas, but the delicate custards, whips, creams, and what the colonel's Hibernian orderly described as "floating Irelands," which that messenger bore with Mrs. Frazier's love, or Miss Frazier's compliments, or Miss 'Manda Frazier's regards and hopes that the

189

captain was better this morning, could be numbered only by the passing days. What Mrs. Frazier was prepared to see or hear of was similar
attention on the part of Mrs. Winn; but Mrs.
Winn's attentions took a form more difficult to
see, and, even in a frontier, old-time garrison, to
hear of.

What Mrs. Frazier was not prepared to see was
Mrs. Blythe in frequent confidential chat with
the officer whom the colonel's wife chose to con-
sider her own invalid. She had always fancied
Mrs. Blythe before, but now she met her with
that indescribable tone suggestive of unmerited
yet meekly, womanfully borne injury, which is
so superior to either explanation or resentment.
Mrs. Winn was frequently on her piazza chatting
with Mr. Brayton or Dr. "Funnybone," as the
wits of the post had designated Collabone's right
bower, "who has more brains in one head," said
Collabone, "than the mess has in ten;" but she
greeted Mrs. Frazier with an austere and distant
dignity even more pronounced than Mrs. Frazier's
manner to Mrs. Blythe, which plainly showed
that Laura had not "been raised in the army for
nothing," and that she had a will and temper and
pluck that would brook no airs and tolerate no
aspersions on Mrs. Frazier's part. Aspersions
there had been, for her friend Mrs. Faulkner had

not failed in that sisterly duty which so many women so reluctantly yet faithfully perform, and everything Mrs. and the Misses Frazier had even hinted, and some things they even hadn't, were duly conveyed to Laura's ears. She was angered at the Fraziers for daring to say such things, at Mrs. Faulkner for daring to repeat them, and at Barclay for daring to keep her beyond the possibility of their being true. Never before had she known what it was to strive for a look or word of admiration and to meet utter indifference. Yet those blue eyes of Barclay's had once fairly burned with passionate delight in her girlish beauty, and his words had trembled with their weight of love for her. No other woman, she believed, had yet come into his life and banished all memory of her; and, now that her beauty was but the riper for her years, she rebelled in her soul against the whisper that it could no longer move him.

Wedded though she was to Harry Winn, loving him after the fashion of her shallow nature so long as there was no man at the post from whom she sought to exact homage, she had time and again within the year felt towards her husband a sense of injury. What business had he had to woo her if he was so poor? What right had he to subject her to the annoyance of dunning let-

ters, of suggestive inquiries on the part of her
neighbors? Why should she submit to parsimo-
nious skimping and cheese-paring, to living with
only one servant when several other women had
two, to all the little shifts and meannesses poor
Harry had declared to be necessary? It was his
business to provide for her needs. Her father
had always supported her in style; why couldn't
Harry do the same? True, she knew when she
married him he had nothing but his pay. He
told her everything, but she had never taken
thought for the morrow, though she had taken
perhaps too much thought of what she should
wear or eat or drink. Laura loved the good things
of this life, and had been freely indulged throughout her petted girlhood; and now, in the days
when every woman seemed turning against her,
purse, cellar, and larder were empty and her husband gone on a stupid foray to the mountains.
None could say when he would return, or what
new sorrow would meet him then. Other men
managed to earn money or make money somehow outside their pay. Why should she, whose
tastes, she said, were so much more refined, be
mated with one who could only spend?

There is a time when many a homely face becomes radiant with a beauty too deep for sallow
skin or heavy features to hide, and when a really

winsome face becomes well-nigh angelic; but,
even as Laura Winn bent over her sleeping child
or nestled the unconscious little one in her bosom,
the sullen fire of discontent, thwarted ambition,
and wounded self-love smouldered in her deep,
slumberous eyes. There were hours now when
Baby Winn was left to the scant care of the
household nurse, while the mother took the air
upon the piazza during the day or flitted about
from parlor to parlor along the row at night. She
was restless, nervous, as all could see. She frequently assailed Brayton with queries for news,
always decorously asking first if couriers had come
or were expected from the command afield, yet
speedily coming back to the real object of her
constant thoughts, the now much honored officer,
her next-door neighbor. For three days after he
was pronounced able to sit up she did not succeed
in seeing him at all, though so many other and,
it should be explained, much older women did;
but that did not abate one whit her determination
that he should speedily see her.

Just what her object was she herself could not
have told. It was an instinct, an impulse, a whim,
perhaps; but he who had been her lover and was
rejected had dared to gaze into her face with eyes
serene and untroubled, had met her but half-
veiled references to old days with polite but posi-

tive indifference. She had nothing to ask of **him**,
she told herself; she meant no disloyalty **to**
Harry, no wrong of any kind. Not a bit of it!
She had treated Barclay very badly. She had
done him a wrong that was much greater in her
own estimation than it was in that of any one of
her neighbors, among whom the women, at least,
considered the loss of his inamorata a blessing in
disguise; but Laura fully believed that Barclay's
heart must have been crushed in the depth of his
woe, and that it was now her duty to make friends
again,—perhaps in some way to console him; not,
of course, in any way to which Harry could object, not, of course, in any way to which the post
ought to object, but—well, even to herself, as has
been said, she could not entirely and satisfactorily
explain her motives; it was impossible, therefore,
that she could hope to do so to anybody else; and
yet she had dared to write to him. It was only
a little note, and yet, with all its inconsistencies,
it said so much:

"DEAR CAPTAIN BARCLAY,—I cannot tell you
my distress at hearing of your again being severely wounded, especially at a time when I had
hoped to have you meet and better know my husband, but now in his distressing absence I, who
more than any woman at this post am anxious to

show my sympathy and sorrow, am practically helpless. Do tell me if there is anything I can do,—though I am sure I can't see what is left for me, with no cook or kitchen, and Mrs. Frazier and the Misses Frazier sending such loads of things. I really envy them and Mrs. Blythe the privilege of their years in going to see you personally, for am I not at least

"Your oldest friend,   "L. W."

This ingenuous note was sent by Hannibal at an hour when the captain was alone, and when, had he been disposed, he might have hobbled to the door and answered in person; but hobble he did not, nor did he answer until after long thought. He received the little missive with surprise, read it without a tremor of hand or lip, but with something of shame and pity that overspread his face like a cloud. Was he only just beginning to know her, after all?

"Pray do not give my scratch a thought," he answered, in writing, late that afternoon, "and believe, my dear Mrs. Winn, that I have every comfort that one can possibly desire. Every one is most kind. I expect to be out with my men in a week, and shall be delighted to take the field and send Mr. Winn back to you forthwith.

"Most sincerely."

And that was how, with polite but positive indifference, he had treated her reference to old
times and old friends. Shallow as she was, Laura
Winn was deep enough to see that he meant to
hold himself far aloof from her. He could hardly
have told her more plainly he would have none
of her. He had even dared to say it would be
a pleasure to go, that he might send her husband
back to her arms. And this was the man she once
thought she loved, the man who, she believed,
adored her and would never outlive the passion
of his sorrow at losing her!

Even now the foolish heart of the woman might
have accepted its lesson; but it was time for
friends again to come, and, as Laura expressed it,
"pry and prod and preach," and that brought on
a climax.

Mrs. Faulkner had dropped in and dropped out
again, and Laura, who seemed forever going to
the porch these days, followed and called her
back.

"One thing you said I don't understand," she
began, and Mrs. Faulkner's pretty face showed
plainly there had been something of a storm.

"I said this, Laura," her friend responded, per-
mitting her to go no further, but turning at the
step and looking up into her indignant eyes.
"You do yourself injury by showing such con-

cern about Captain Barclay. Everybody says so, and it's all wasted as far as he's concerned. He never notices your messages in any way."

It was galling to feel herself censured or criticised, but Mrs. Winn was becoming used to that. It was worse than galling to be told that her whilom lover now turned from her almost with contempt. She could bear it that they should say that Galahad Barclay was again circling within danger of her fascinations and would speedily find himself powerless to resist. She could not bear it that they should declare him dead to her. The anger ablaze in her eyes and flushing her cheeks was something even Mrs. Faulkner had never seen before. It was as though she had roused some almost tigerish trait. For a moment Laura stood glaring at her visitor, one hand nervously clutching at the balcony rail, the other at the snugly buttoned bodice of her dark gown. At that instant the door of Barclay's quarters opened and the sound of glad voices preceded but a second or two the appearance of feminine drapery at the threshold. Mrs. Brooks came backing into view, chatting volubly with some one still invisible. Mrs. Frazier came sidling after, and then as they reached the open air the deep tones of their invalid host were heard mingling with the lighter, shriller, if not exactly

silvery accents of his visitors. One glance they
threw towards the young matron at the opposite
end of the piazza, and then it seemed as though
Mrs. Frazier promptly precipitated herself into
the doorway again, as though to block it against
Barclay's possible egress. "Determined not to
let him see me, nor me him," were the unspoken
words that flashed through Laura's thoughts.
Some devil of mischief seemed to whisper in her
ear, for when Mrs. Faulkner turned again, there
stood her hostess holding forth for her inspection
a little note addressed to Mrs. H. H. Winn in a
hand Mrs. Faulkner recognized at once as that
of Barclay. With an icy sneer the irate lady
spoke:

"You think he doesn't write. This came only
an hour ago."

Not five minutes later Mrs. Frazier turned to
Mrs. Faulkner and asked, "What was Laura
Winn showing you?—a letter?"

Mrs. Blythe was passing at the moment, Ada
Lawrence, a tall, pallid slip of a girl, in her first
black dress, walking sadly at her side. Mrs.
Faulkner nodded assent to the question, but
glanced significantly at the passers-by, on their
way seemingly to the house the elders had just
left. Mrs. Blythe bowed courteously and smiled,
but the smile was one of those half-hearted at-

tempts that seemed to wither instantly at Mrs.
Frazier's solemn and distant salutation.

"Now what's that woman taking Ada Lawrence there for?" was Mrs. Frazier's query the
instant the two were out of earshot, and for the
moment she forgot the letter and the significant
glance in Mrs. Faulkner's eyes. But Mrs. Brooks
had not, and no sooner had the door of Barclay's
quarters opened and swallowed up the new callers
than the major's wife turned back to it.

"You don't mean a letter from—*him?*" she
asked, with a nod of the head at Barclay's quarters.

"I didn't mean to say anything about it," said
Mrs. Faulkner, with proper hesitation, "but you
seem to know as much as I do, and she made no
secret of it whatever. Indeed, I don't know that
there's anything in it that anybody mightn't see."

"I think she has no business whatever receiving letters now that her husband's away—nor any
other time, for that matter," said Mrs. Frazier,
hotly; "and I mean to tell her so; and I'm astonished at him."

"For heaven's sake don't tell her I let it out!"
exclaimed Mrs. Faulkner. "You've just got to
say you saw it away from his door."

"Well, I think the sooner Mr. Harry Winn
gets back the better it will be for this garrison,

and I'll say so to Colonel Frazier this very night,"
exclaimed the colonel's wife, bristling with proper
indignation. "And he'll come back, if we have
to send couriers to order him."

But no courier was needed to summon Lieutenant Winn. Two days later, fast as jaded horse
could carry him, followed by a single orderly, he
was coming, full of hope and pluck and enthu-
siasm, the bearer of tidings that meant so much
to him, that might be of such weight in the re-
moval of some portion, at least, of the serious
stoppages against his pay. Away out in the
Apache mountains, where the remnants of the
Friday gang seemed to have scattered into little
squads of two or three, one party had been trailed
and chased to its hole, a wild nook in the rocks,
and there in brief, bloody fight two more of the
gang bit the dust in reaching that height of
outlaw ambition, "dying with their boots on."
Others were wounded and captured, and still
another, neither wounded nor combatant, but a
trembling skulker, was dragged out from a cleft
in among the boulders and kicked into the presence of the commanding officer by a burly Irishman who would have lost the bliss of a dozen
pay-day sprees rather than that one achievement,
for the skulking captive was Marsden, and Marsden was English.

A more abject, pitiable, helpless wretch even
Texan troopers had never seen. Imploring his
captors to protect him against the illimitable pos-
sibilities of lynch law,—for there were veteran
soldiers present to whose thinking drum-head
court-martial and summary execution were all too
good for Marsden,—the ex-sergeant told the
story of his stealings, and the names of his accom-
plices, but declared that all his ill-gotten gains
were gone. Every cent he had at the time of
his flight was taken from him, he protested, by the
gang of desperadoes among whom he had found
refuge.

"He's lyin', sorr," declared Sergeant Shaugh-
nessy at this juncture. "He's hidin' the hoith av
it somewheres, an' there's nothin' like the noose
av a lariat to frishen his mimory." But old Mullane ordered silence.

"Go you back to Worth fast as you can," said
he to Winn. "Write the report for me to sign
before you start. Tell the colonel where what is
left of the stolen property can be found, and we'll
bring Marsden along with us. The quicker you
get there the more you can save."

Worth was one hundred and fifty miles away
on a bee-line, and Winn had to twist and turn,
but he rode with buoyant heart. By prompt
measures much of his misfortune might be wiped

out. Then, with the proffered loan with which to settle his accounts and pay off certain pressing creditors, he could start afresh, his head at last above the waters that had weighed him down. He would lead a simple, inexpensive life, and Laura would have to help him. He could set aside one-fourth, or even, perhaps, one-third, of his pay to send each month to the bank at San Antonio. It would be hard, but at least he would be honest and manful, and Laura would have to try to dress and live inexpensively. She used to say she would rather share exile and poverty with him than a palace with any other man, but that seemed a bit like hyperbole in the light of her subsequent career. Long before this, he said, the bank would have sent the money to Worth. It was doubtless now awaiting him in Fuller's safe, or possibly Trott's. How blessed a thing it was that the cashier should have been an old and warm friend of his father,—that he should have written proffering aid for old times' sake to the son of the soldier he had known and been aided by and had learned to love in bygone days! It was odd that Mr. Cashier Bolton had not made himself known to him, Harry Winn, when he and his lovely bride were in San Antonio, but all the more was the offer appreciated. It was odd that he should couple with the offer a condition that Winn should give his word not to tell the name of his father's friend and his own bene-factor, and further to agree neither to drink any intoxicant nor bet a cent on any game of chance until the money was repaid. He was not given to drinking, but he had heard of a fondness on his father's part for cards, and had felt the fas-cination himself. All right: he would promise gladly.

They got fresh horses at a midway camp where a small detachment guarded the Cougar Springs, rested during the hot hours of the first day after a long night ride, then set forth, chasing their long shadows in the late afternoon, and, riding on through the night, hove in sight of the twinkling lights in the company kitchens at Worth just as the dawn was spreading over the eastward prairie. At the guard-house, aroused by the sentry's warn-ing, a sergeant tumbled off his bench and ran sleepily out to meet them. It was a man whom Winn had frequently seen hovering about his quarters in attendance upon their maid-of-all-work.

"All well at home, Quigley?" he queried, hope-fully.

"All well, sir; leastwise Mrs. Winn and the baby is, so Miss Purdy said yesterday evenin'. Mrs. Blythe with her children and Colonel Lawrence's have gone to San Antonio. They're all goin' home together. Any luck, sir?"

"I should say so! Hit 'em hard twice, and caught Marsden alive."

"Great——— Beg pardon, lieutenant, but that's the best news yet!" The soldier's eyes danced and pleaded for more, but Winn was eager to reach home, to tiptoe up to Laura's room, to kneel by the bedside and fold her, waking, in his strong, yearning arms, to bend and kiss his baby's sleeping face. He spurred on across the parade. The long, low line of officers' quarters lay black and unrelieved against the reddening sky. Only in one or two were faint night-lights burning, one down near the southern end, the room of the officer of the day, another in his own. The slats of the blinds, half turned, revealed the glimmer of a lamp within. Probably baby was awake and demanding entertainment, and there could be no surprising Laura as he had planned. Still, he guided his horse so as to avoid pebbles or anything that would click against the shod hoofs. The home-coming would be the sweeter for its being unheralded.

"Never mind the saddle-bags now," he murmured to his orderly. "Take the horses to stables, and bring the traps over by and by." Then he tiptoed around to the back of the house.

The front door, he knew, would be locked; so
would that opening on the little gallery in rear;
but there was the window of his den; he could
easily raise it from outside and let himself in
without any one's being the wiser. A glance at
his watch showed him that in ten minutes the
morning gun would fire and the post wake up to
the shrill reveille of the infantry fifes and drums.
Even though Laura should be awake and up with
her baby, the surprise might be attempted. The
back porch was lighted up with the glow from
the east. The back door of the Barclay-Brayton
establishment was ajar, and some one was moving
about in the kitchen,—Hannibal, probably, getting coffee for his master in time for morning
stables. Just to try it, Winn tiptoed up the low
steps to the rear door, and there it stood, not wide
open, but just ajar. "Miss Purdy" had mended
her ways, then, and was rising betimes, he said.
Softly entering, he passed through the little
kitchen into the dark dining-room beyond, felt
his way through into his deserted den to the left,
—the blinds were tightly closed,—thence to the
narrow hall, and up the carpeted, creaking stairs.
The door of the back room at the east, the nur-
sery, was right at the landing. The light of the
dawn was strong enough to reveal dimly objects
within. That door, too, was wide open, and there

by the bedside was the cradle of his baby, and
the little one placidly asleep. There in her bed,
innocent of the possibility of masculine observa-
tion, her ears closed, her mouth wide open in the
stupor of sleep, lay the domestic combination of
nurse and maid-of-all-work. He tiptoed past the
door and softly approached that of the front, the
westward room,—his and Laura's. It, too, was
partly open. A lamp burned dimly on the bu-
reau. The broad, white bed, with its tumbled
pillows and tossed-back coverlet, was empty, as
he found the room to be. Laura, then, and not
the maid, was the early riser. Softly he searched
about the upper floor. She had heard him, after
all, and was hiding somewhere to tease him. No;
there on the back of her rocking-chair hung the
pink, beribboned wrapper that was so becoming
to her, and on another the dainty, lace-trimmed
night-robe. She must be up and dressed,—his
languid, lazy Laura, who rarely rose before nine
o'clock, as a rule, and now it was only five. A
strange throbbing began at his heart. Quickly
he turned and scurried down the stairs, struck a
match in the parlor, another in the dining-room.
Both were empty. The den and its closets were
explored. No one there.

Out he went through the kitchen to the eastward porch again. The light was stronger. Over

the level *mesa* to the edge of the bluff, not fifty
yards away, his eager eyes swept in search of the
truant form. There stood at the very brow of
the projecting point at the northeast side a little,
latticed summer-house where sentimental couples
sometimes sat and looked over the shallow valley
of moonlight nights; and there, close beside it,
switching the skirt of her stylish riding-habit with
her whip, stood Laura Winn. Just as she turned
and glanced impatiently over her shoulder, out
from the adjoining door came a soldierly form in
riding-dress. For an instant three forms seemed
to stand stock-still; then came the shock and roar
of the reveille gun, and before the echoes rolled
away Lieutenant Winn, striding up to Barclay
with fury in his eyes, struck the captain full in
the face and sent him crashing over a kitchen
chair.

CHAPTER XV.

TEN miles out to the northwest the stream that curved and twisted around the low *mesa* of Fort Worth burst its way through a ridge in the foothills, and, brawling and dashing at its rocky banks, rolled out over the lowlands, foaming at the mouth with the violence of its own struggles. Far in the heart of the hills it had its source in several clear, cold springs, while the deep hoarded snows of the harsh winters fed and swelled it in the springtide until it reached the proportions of a short-lived torrent. Huge heaps of uprooted trees and tangled brushwood it deposited along its shores as far down even as the fort, but nothing was carried below the sutler's. "Ahl's fish that comes to Fuller's net," said Sergeant McHugh, "an' sorra a sliver av a sardine iver got away from it." Once in a while, after unusual flood, the flotsam and jetsam of the creek would be diversified with wagon-bodies, ranch roofs, camp equipage, and the like, for "the Range," as this odd upheaval was locally termed, was a famous place for prospectors.

A beautiful stream was the Blanca within its

mountain gates, but an ashen pallor overspread it after its fight for freedom. It was never the same stream after it got away. It danced and sparkled past pretty nooks and shaded ravines among the hills, but issued from the gateway, like the far-famed Stinking River of the Bannocks and Shoshones of Northwestern Wyoming, a metamorphosed stream. It had a bad reputation. It was solely responsible for the fact that Worth had been located away out here in the bald, bleak, open prairie country, instead of among those bold and beautiful heights to the northwest. "The very spot for a military post!" said the officers of the earlier scouting parties, as they camped within the gates in the midst of a lonely glade. "Lovely," said the Texan guides, in reply, "so long as you don't mind being drowned out every spring." It seems that snows would melt of a sudden, tremendous thunderstorms burst among the crags, and flood and deluge the valleys, for the Blanca could not with sufficient swiftness discharge its swollen torrents through that narrow gorge. Beautiful it lay, ordinarily, as a summer sea, and the bridle-path that wound through the pass was a favorite route for picnic-parties from Worth. But storm-clouds would rise and turn summer seas to raging water-demons, and then the flood that tore through the gates would sweep all before it, like the unloosed waters of the Conemaugh that awful May of '89.

From Worth to the White Gate the prairie road wound hard and firm, and before the late excitement several picnic-, riding-, and driving-parties had paid their spring-time visits. It was quite the thing, too, for such maids and matrons as were good horsewomen to ride thither in the lengthening afternoons. Mrs. Frazier had consulted Collabone as to the earliest date on which Barclay could stand a long drive, as she wished to give a little *fête* in his honor, and had planned a picnic to Barrier Rock, a romantic spot just within the gorge. Collabone had referred her to his assistant, and that younger officer consulted his patient before committing himself to reply.

"I don't care to ride in an ambulance, doctor, but I do long to get in saddle. There's no strain on that leg below the knee. Can't you let me mount from my back porch here and amble around these fine mornings before people are up?" And "Funnybone" assented. He and Barclay rode out together, very cautiously, next morning at reveille, and, finding his patient benefited by the gentle exercise on such a perfect mount as either of those Kentucky bays, the doctor said, "Go again; only ride slowly, and mount and dismount only at the back porch, where you have only to lower yourself into saddle. Be sure to avoid any shock or jar, then you're all right."

Hannibal and Mrs. Winn's domestic were the only persons besides Barclay's orderly to see the start, but had the domestic herself been alone it would have been sufficient to insure transmission of the news. First she told her mistress. Later she learned from Hannibal that the captain was going out to stables next morning the same way, and had ordered coffee to be ready at reveille. This, too, was conveyed to Laura, and that evening she sent for the veteran stable sergeant of the troop to which her husband was temporarily attached, and asked him if Robin Hood, a pretty little chestnut she used to ride, was still in the stable. He was, and would Mrs. Winn be pleased to ride? The sergeant would be glad to see the lady in saddle again. Her handsome side-saddle was, with her bridle, always kept in perfect order, but for several months Mrs. Winn had taken no exercise that way.

"I'm going to ride at reveille, sergeant," she confided to the faithful soldier. "It's so long since I mounted, I wish to try once or twice when people can't see me." And Sergeant Burns had promised that as soon as the sentry would release him after gun-fire Robin Hood should be on hand. He'd be proud to come with him himself.

True to his word, Burns was up at four-fifteen; Robin was groomed and fed and watered and saddled in style, and ready to start the moment the sentry was relieved by the morning gun-fire from the imposition of the order to "allow no horse to be taken out between taps and reveille, except in the presence of a commissioned officer or the sergeant of the guard." The sight that met the sergeant's eyes as he cantered around back of the row of officers' quarters, leading Robin by the rein, was one he never forgot.

With pallid face, down which the blood was streaming from a cut at the temple, Captain Barclay was seated on the steps, striving to bind a handkerchief about his lower leg. Old Hannibal, forgetful of the dignity of the Old Dominion, was actually running down the back road, in haste, it seems, to summon the doctor. On the porch, amid some overturned chairs, two athletic, sinewy young men were grappling, one of them, Lieutenant Brayton, almost lifting and carrying the other, Lieutenant Winn, towards his own doorway, both ashen gray as to their faces, both fearfully excited, both struggling hard, both with panting breath striving to speak with exaggerated calm.

On this scene, wringing her hands, sobbing with fright and misery, flitting first to Barclay's

side, then back towards her straining husband,
saying wild and incoherent things to both, was
Laura Winn. Burns had the frontiersman's contempt for a chimney-pot hat, and never seemed
one so incongruous as this,—her riding head-gear
which in the midst of her wailings Mrs. Winn
clasped to her heaving breast. To make matters
more complicated, the neighborhood was waking
up, domestics and "strikers" were gazing from
back porches farther down the row, and Blythe's
big hounds had taken to barking furiously, until
that bulky and bewildered soldier himself came
forth, damned them into their kennel, then hastened in consternation to the aid of Barclay. By
this time, too, Winn had succeeded in making his
wife hear him, and was ordering her within-doors;
but like some daft creature she hovered, moaning
and wringing her hands and staring at Barclay,
whose eyes were now beginning to close, and
whose form was slowly swaying.

"In God's name, man, what's happened?" demanded Blythe, as he seized and steadied the
toppling form. "Why, you're bleeding like an
ox. Your boot is running over. Drop those
horses, Burns, and run for the doctor, lively," he
urged. Needing no further authority, the sergeant turned his charges loose and scurried after
Hannibal.

"Help me carry Barclay in-doors," was the next word. With one warning order to Winn to keep away, young Brayton broke loose from him and ran to assist. As though half stupefied, Winn heavily moved a pace or two, then sank upon a bench and stared. His wife stood gazing in horror at the trail of blood that followed the three men into the hall, then faltered over to where the young soldier sat, moaning, "Oh, Harry! Oh, Harry!" Reaching his side, she laid her hand upon his shoulder and bade him look at her,—speak to her. He rose slowly to his feet, his face averted, shook himself free, and, with a shudder, but never uttering a word in reply, passed into his dark doorway. The nurse-girl, wide-eyed, met him at the threshold. "Go to your mistress," he said, hoarsely. He stumbled on through the house, unslung the revolver belted to his waist, and laid it on the hall table; reconsidered; buckled it firmly on, and, pulling his hat down over his eyes, drew back the door-bolt and let himself out upon the front piazza. Crossing the parade, he saw the red sash of the officer of the day. De Lancy was dragging sleepily back from his reveille visit to the guard, but the sight of Winn aroused him, and he quickened his pace and came striding to him.

"Hullo, lad," he hailed, full twenty paces

away, "what luck? Got Marsden, the sergeant
tells me.—Why—— Good God! what's happened?"

"Nothing," said Winn, "except, perhaps, I've
killed Barclay. Take me to the colonel."

"You're daft, man!" said De Lancy, instantly,
while an awful fear almost checked the beating
of his heart. Then, seizing Winn by the arm,
"What d'ye mean?" he asked.

"Go and see," said Winn, stupidly, as he
buried his face in his arms a moment, then
stretched them out full length, and, tossing his
head back, shut his eyes as though to blot out a
hateful sight. "Go," he continued; "then come
and take me to the colonel."

And De Lancy started on the run and collided
with Brayton at the door.

"For God's sake, go and hurry up 'Funnybone,'" moaned the youngster. "Here's Barclay
bleeding to death."

De Lancy ran his best: guardsmen across the
parade stopped and stared, men in shirt-sleeves
rushed out on the barrack stoops and stood and
gazed, and a corporal, with rifle trailed, came
running over to see what was amiss, just as the
junior doctor, in cap and overcoat, trousers and
slippers, came bolting out of his hallway and flying up the path. In front of De Lancy's one

slipper went hurtling back through midair, but
the doctor rushed on in stocking-foot. The corporal picked up the shoe and followed. No one
seemed to look for the moment at Winn, who
turned slowly back to the pathway and like a
blind man seemed groping his way towards Frazier's. The officer of the day passed him by on
the run, following at the doctor's heels, with
never another look at him. Men seemed to think
only of Barclay. Was it credible that an officer
and a gentleman, as Winn had been regarded,
could purposely have dealt that honored soldier a
mortal blow, unless—unless—but who could find
words to frame the thought? Once within Brayton's hallway, De Lancy turned and slammed shut
the door, for others were coming on the run from
far across the parade. Over at the guard-house
the men had started for their breakfast, but hung
there, clustered about the sentry-post, gazing over
the criss-cross plat of the parade, and muttering
their conjectures as to the cause of the trouble.
The sight of Lieutenant Winn wandering on
down the row, turning from time to time, halting
as though uncertain what he ought to do, while
every other officer was running to the other end
of the row, was something they could not understand.

Then Mrs. Winn, in riding-habit, came sud-

denly forth upon her piazza, and, gazing wildly
up and down, caught sight of her husband, now
some fifty paces away along the gravel walk.
Stretching forth her arms to him, she began to
call aloud, "Harry! Harry! please come back!"
He never turned. She ran down the steps and out
to the gate and called him, louder, louder, so that
they could hear the voice all over the garrison in
the sweet, still morning air; but on he went, doggedly now, faster and faster. She gathered up
her clinging skirts in one hand, and, pleading still,
followed after. Not until he had mounted the
steps at the colonel's did the young officer turn
again; then with uplifted hand and arm he stood
warning her back. Something in the attitude,
something in the stern, quivering white face,
seemed at last to bring to her the realization of
the force of his unspoken denunciation.

"Harry! Harry!" she cried. "Oh, come and
let me tell you. You don't understand! I meant
no wrong! I was only going for a ride,—not with
him,—not with him, Harry!" And so, pleading,
weeping, she followed almost to the colonel's gate
before the door was opened from within and
Winn was swallowed up in the darkness of the
hall.

By this time some inkling of the trouble had
been borne to Collabone, ever an early riser. As

he came hastily forth from his quarters, the first
thing he saw was the drooping form of Mrs.
Winn, weeping at the colonel's gate. Seizing her
arm with scant ceremony, he whirled her about
and bore her homeward, she sobbing out her story
as they sped along, he listening with clouded,
anxious face.

"Go back to your room, Mrs. Winn," he said,
so solemnly and warningly she could not but heed.
"Go to your baby. I'll go first next door, then
I'll find your husband." She shrank within the
hallway, and threw herself, weeping miserably,
upon the sofa in the pretty parlor,—the parlor
where she had so fascinated Hodge. There the
sound of her baby's wailing reached her in an
interval of her own, and she called to the nurse
to do something to comfort that child. There was
no answer. "Miss Purdy," with clattering tongue
and eager eyes and ears and half a dozen sympathizing neighbors, was out in rear of the house,
deaf to demands of either mother or child; there
Collabone found her, and sent her scurrying
within before the fury of his wrath.

"Now, this will not do, Mrs. Winn," he said,
as, following, he lifted the moaning woman from
the sofa. "You must go to your room,—to your
child, as I told you. Captain Barclay will soon be
all right. He has lost much blood, but the hemor-

rhage is checked. Now I will go for Mr. Winn. It's a bad business, but don't make it worse by any more—nonsense." With that he not too gently pushed her up the first few stairs, then turned abruptly and hastened away to Frazier's.

In the hall he found that gray-haired, gray-faced veteran listening stupidly to Winn.

"I don't understand, sir," he was saying. "You struck him—with what?"

"I don't know," said Winn. "They say I've killed him. I have come to surrender myself." His eyes were as dull and leaden as his heart.

"It's not so bad," burst in the doctor. "Barclay fell or was knocked over a chair, and the jar reopened his wound. He fainted from loss of blood, but it's checked now."

"But—how?—why?" the colonel was stammering. Over the balustrade aloft popped one head night-capped, and two with touseled hair, and blanched faces were framed in all three, and gasping words were heard, and whisperings as of awe-stricken, news-craving souls. "Where did this occur, and when did you return, sir?"

"On the back porch of my—of our quarters, colonel,—when I got back, just before gun-fire."

"And what possible excuse or explanation have you, sir? What could warrant such—such conduct?" demanded Frazier, as though at a loss for suitable words. Yet, even as he asked, his wife's predictions reasserted themselves, and he glanced uneasily aloft.

"Come into the parlor, colonel," implored Collabone. "Say no more here. Let me explain. It's all a wretched mistake." And, half pushing, half pulling, but all impelling, the doctor succeeded in hustling the post commander and the inert, unresisting subaltern within the parlor. Then, to the infinite disgust of the colonel's wife, he shut—yes, slammed—the door.

A quarter of an hour later, in close arrest, Lieutenant Winn returned to his own roof and locked himself in his den. Mrs. Winn, kneeling at the keyhole, pleaded ten minutes for admission, all in vain; then she sent her maid for Dr. Collabone and Mrs. Faulkner, and went straightway to bed.

CHAPTER XVI.

THREE days more, and back came Mullane with the wretched prisoner Marsden. The Irish captain's eyes grew saucer-big when he heard the harrowing details of recent events at the post. Never in its liveliest days, before or since, had Worth known an excitement to match this; for, with the best intentions in the world, there wasn't a woman in officers' row who could.get at the bottom facts of the episode. Rumors of the wildest kind that were early in circulation were best left to the imagination of the reader. The only thing actually known was that Mrs. Winn and Captain Barclay were going out riding at reveille, that Winn surprised them and knocked the captain down, that Winn was now in close arrest, Barclay on the mend and again sitting up, Mrs. Winn confined by illness to her bed, Mrs. Faulkner (a most important person she) in devoted attendance, all their differences forgiven if not forgotten,—and there were few Mrs. Faulkner would not have forgiven for the bliss of being for the time the most sought-after woman at Worth, for every one wanted to know how Mrs.

Winn was every hour of the day, and hoped to
hear what dreadful imprudence of hers it was
that caused the equally dreadful fracas.

Gravely and quietly the doctors told their story
to the colonel; that there was no arrangement or
engagement to ride together; that Captain Barclay had no idea Mrs. Winn ever rose—much less
rode—that early; and most men accepted the
statement as true.   But there was the fatal exhibition of Barclay's letter by Mrs. Winn to con-
front the women, who would have held him guilt-
less and saddled all the blame upon her lovely,
sloping shoulders.   What had he to write to her
about, unless it was to ask her to ride or something
of the kind?   And the idea of their daring to
select such an hour, instead of going out when—
when people could see!   And then there was the
fact that Mr. Winn still refused to be reconciled
to his wife.   What did that mean, if not that he
deemed her guilty?   Blythe, who had a kindlier
feeling for Winn than had most men at Worth
(for Brayton now was utterly set against him and
refused to go near him), sent in his card and
begged to be allowed to see him; and Blythe's
face was sad and gray when, half an hour later,
he came forth again.

"Colonel," said he to Frazier, "something has
got to be done for that poor fellow, or he'll go

mad. Collabone has told him Barclay was totally
ignorant of Mrs. Winn's plan to ride that morning,—that his assault was utterly unjustifiable;
and between that and the contemplation of his
wife's brainless freak, and all his old trouble, I'm
sorely afraid he'll break down,—go all to pieces.
Can't something be done?"

Both Frazier and Brooks thought something
ought to be done; and so said Blythe and De
Lancy, and Follansbee and Fellows, when they
came trooping home, empty-handed, from their
scout. Only Mullane's detachment had accomplished anything, and such success as he had was
due almost entirely to Winn's persistent effort and
energetic trailing. Something was being done to
hunt up stolen stores as revealed by Marsden, but
poor Winn, who had ridden home so full of hope
and pluck and energy, now paced his narrow
room for hours, or lay upon his lounge, face
buried in his arms, either dull and apathetic or
smarting with agony. On Mrs. Winn old Collabone had little sympathy to waste. Bluntly he
told her that she was responsible for the whole
business and deserved to be down sick. So, too,
he told the colonel, who was having a blissful
time answering the questions and squirming under the nagging of his household at home. At
first Laura had shown tremendous spirit. Mr.

Winn's conduct was an insult. The doctor's comments were an insult. The instant she was well
enough to move she would take her precious child
and return to her mother's roof.

"Your mother hasn't any roof," said Collabone. "She's boarding in Washington, playing
for another husband, and you'd spoil the whole
game, turning up with a grandchild. What
you've got to do is beg your husband's pardon for
all the scrapes you've led him into,—this last one
especially." Laura wailed and wept and cried out
against the heartless cruelty of her husband, who
left her sick and dying, for all he knew (Collabone had assured him there was nothing on earth
the matter but nerves), and she thought Mrs.
Faulkner ought to *make* him hear how ill she was.
At last she managed to have herself appropriately
arrayed, and with face of meekest suffering way-
laid him on the lower floor before he could close
the door against her, after a brief official visit
from the adjutant.

But the first glance into his haggard, hopeless
face, the sight of despair such as she had never
dreamed of, struck to her soul something like ter-
ror. One moment she gazed, all thought of her
puny troubles vanished and forgotten, and then
with one great cry—the first genuine feeling she
had shown—the unhappy woman threw herself at

his feet and clasped her arms about his trembling knees.

That night when the doctor called he found her humbled, contrite, concerned in earnest, and all for her husband. "It's the first time," said he, "I've ever felt any respect for you whatever, Mrs. Winn. I believe there's something in you, after all,"—"though probably not much," he later added when he told his wife. That night, too, he and Brooks and Blythe sat half an hour with Winn. The colonel asked them to do it, for it was time to help him if help was to come at all. The same day brought inquiry from Department Head-Quarters as to whether Lieutenant Winn had made good the amount of that great shortage; and the promised money package had not come.

Gently they asked him if he had reasonable right to look for it, and all the answer he could make was that it had been promised on certain conditions. He had recently accepted them, had expected to find the money on his arrival at Worth, but instead had found—— and the hands thrown hopelessly forward, palms upraised, were as expressive as any words could have been. There was silence a moment. Then he spoke again.

"And, after all, what matters it now? With

this court-martial hanging over me, I've nothing but dismissal from the army to look forward to in any event."

"And what if there should be no trial, Winn?" said the major, after a reflective pause. "It is true that you have made an awful—break; but as yet you are your only accuser, and Mrs. Winn is the only witness, for Barclay is dumb."

But Winn shook his head. "I know enough of army matters to know that this thing is all over the post and will soon be all over Texas. If Captain Barclay was of—the old army,—if he had been brought up as I was, we might settle it out of court. My father used to say that there could be no other reparation for a blow. What would my apologies be worth? They would not re-establish him."

"Sometimes I think," said Brooks, after another reflective pause, "that men of Barclay's stamp need no appeal to the code to set them right. That is only a device by which physical courage is made a substitute for other virtues that may be lacking. Barclay occupies a plane above it. In view of his record in the Platte country and in this recent chase after the outlaws, it would take a bold man to sneer at him, in this garrison at least; and if he prefer no charge against you, who is to do it? This trouble can be straightened out, Winn," said the major, soothingly, "if only you could fix—that other."

But how, said they to each other, as they went gloomily away, was that other to be "fixed"? How was a poor fellow with nothing but his pay, burdened by an extravagant and helpless wife, a little child, and a number of debts, to hope to raise three thousand dollars to prevent the almost total stoppage of his stipend? That evening when Mrs. Faulkner left her invalid friend the latter asked her to say to Harry that she begged him to come and speak with her. Harry went, but there was no spring, no gladness, in the slow and halting feet that climbed the narrow stair; there was no hope in the care-worn face that came forth again in half an hour. Laura wished him to take her watch, her diamond ear-rings, a locket he had given her in bygone days, and other pretty trinkets, sell them, and pay their debts: she was amazed to hear, not that they owed so much, but that her treasures would bring so little.

The fourth day of his arrest was well-nigh gone. Collabone had reported Barclay quite himself again, and sitting up, though none too strong, and then he saw that Winn at last had been writing. "Read that," said Harry, briefly, and handed him the sheet. It was addressed to Captain Barclay.

"In the last four days I have done nothing but

think of the great wrong I did you. I have tried
to find words in which to tell you my distress and
self-reproach, but they fail me. There was no
shadow of justification for my suspicion, and
therefore no excuse for my blow. Had you desired reparation you would have demanded it, and
the rule used to be for a man in my plight to wait
until it was asked before he tendered an apology
that might be considered a stopper to a challenge.
But I will not wait. At the risk of anything any
man may say or think, I write this to tell you that
I deplore my conduct and with all my heart to
beg your pardon."

Collabone went through it twice with blinking
eyes. "That's the bravest thing you ever did,
Winn," said he, as he laid it carefully down.
"That ought to stop court-martial proceedings."

"That," answered Winn, "is a different matter. I don't ask any mercy. I would have been
better off this minute if he or Brayton had shot
me on the spot."

There was silence a moment as he turned away
and presently seated himself at the little table, his
head dropping forward on his arms. Then Collabone stepped up and placed a hand upon his
shoulder.

"Winn, my boy, I should lie if I said you ought
not to feel this, but there's such a thing as brood-

ing too much. You'll harm yourself if you go
on like this. You—— Here! let me take that
in to Barclay. Let him speak for me; I'm
damned if it isn't too much for me!"

But Winn's head was never lifted as the doctor
went his way.

Later that night the post adjutant dropped in.
He and Winn had never been on cordial terms,
but the staff officer was shocked and troubled at
the increasing ravages in the once proud and
handsome face of the cavalryman. "Winn," he
said, in courteous tone, "the colonel directs exten-
sion of your limits to include the parade, and—
and to visit Captain Barclay, who wants to see
you this evening, if you feel able. It's only next
door, you know," he added, vaguely. Then,
"Isn't there anything I can do?"

That night just after taps old Hannibal admitted the tall young officer, and ushered him
into a brightly lighted room, where, rather pale
and wan, but with a kindly smile on his face,
Galahad Barclay lay back in his reclining chair,
and held out a thin, white hand.

"Welcome, Winn," was all he said, and then
the old negro slid out and closed the door.

"There are Oirish and Oirish," as, quoting
Mulvaney, has been said before. Once assured

that no further proceedings were to be taken against him for his iniquitous lapse the day of the rush to Crockett Springs, Captain Mullane concluded that he must stand high in favor at court and that further self-denial and abstinence were uncalled for, especially in view of the successes achieved for him by the small detachment of his party led by Lieutenant Winn. Mullane was a gallant soldier in the field, from sheer love of fighting, and the same trait when warmed by whiskey made him a nuisance in garrison. Not a week was he home from his successful scout when he broke out in a new place, and this time he found instant accommodation.

Little of the stolen property was recovered by the searching squad sent out as the result of Marsden's revelations. That voluble scoundrel was in the guard-house, awaiting trial by general court-martial. Cavalry drills were resumed again, and after each morning's work the officers gathered in considerable force at the club-room. There had been, both in the infantry and in the cavalry, vast speculation as to the outcome of Winn's arrest and Barclay's mishap. But men, as a rule, spoke of the matter with bated breath. Mullane, Bralligan, and the one or two Irish ex-sergeants in the command, known locally as the Faugh-a-Ballaghs, however, waxed hilariously insolent in their comments. Nothing short of dismissal should be Winn's sentence, and nothing short of a challenge be Barclay's course. It was with something akin to amaze that Mullane received on the sixth day after Winn's arrest official notification of his release and restoration to duty. It was with something akin to incredulous wrath that an hour later he caught sight of the liberated lieutenant issuing from Barclay's quarters, not his own, and with Barclay leaning trustfully on his arm.

Apology accepted! Explanations tendered! All settled, and without a meeting on the field of honor! "Whurroo! but hwat's the cavalry comin' to?" howled Mullane over the consequent cups at the sutler's store and club-room, Fuller aiding and abetting with more liquor. Up the hill to the post lurched the big captain that very afternoon, and into the card-room where some of his cronies were gathered, Bralligan among them, and the untrustworthy Hodge. Any one with half an eye could see there was mischief in the wind, for nothing caused these old-time Hibernian rankers keener suffering than to have their betters settle a question without either court-martial or a fight. Talk and jeering laugh grew louder as potations followed on the heel-taps of their predecessors. The mail from San Antonio got in at five P.M. that evening, and the orderly was distributing letters as the officers returned from stables. Winn, by invitation, had accompanied the major, and was walking home with him, Mullane and a crony or two following at safe distance. Several men saw the light of relief in Winn's face as he received, opened, and glanced into the missive handed him.

"Has it come?" asked Brooks, in genuine sympathy.

"Yes," answered Winn, almost solemnly. "A check which I am instructed to have cashed by Fuller, as he has all the currency in the county just now."

"I congratulate you with all my heart," said the major. "I suppose you will see Trott to-morrow."

"I shall see him to-night, if you will excuse me, sir. I'll go at once to the store.—Brayton, will you come with me?"

Fuller was out. It was some minutes before he could be found at the corral. Meantime the two classmates, reconciled since the long talk between Barclay and Winn, conversed in low, grave tones in Fuller's private card-room, where none but officers and his cronies were admitted. "The trader looked queer," said Brayton, "when he took the check," but after some fumbling at his

safe came back with a thick package of treasury
notes, carefully counted out and labelled. On this
display of wealth gloated the fishy eyes of Mullane as a moment later he came reeling in, Bralligan and Hodge at his heels.

To his hilarious salutation Brayton gave short
answer, Winn none at all. Winn's face had
clouded again, and all the sad lines of thought
and care seemed cutting deep, despite the coming
of this much-needed relief.

"Hwat's ahl the lucre, I say?" shouted the
Irish captain, raging at Winn's tacit snub.
"Thousands of dollars, bedad!" Then with leering wink he turned to his half-muddled satellites.
"D'ye mind, lads?—ahl that for a plasther to
wounded honor,—regular John Bull business
over again. That's the English way of settlin' a
crim. con. case. How much did Barclay think it
wurrth, Winn?"

And the next instant he lay floundering on the
floor, felled by a furious blow from the subaltern's
fist.

CHAPTER XVII.

ANOTHER week opened. In honor of Captain Barclay's restoration to health, the Fraziers had issued invitations for a picnic to the White Gate. Many of the officers and ladies had accepted. Most of them had been bidden. Captain Mullane had been on sick report four days,—contusions resulting from tumbling from a broken-legged chair, was the explanation; but every Pat in the command had his tongue in his cheek when he spoke of it, and of matters growing out of the "contusions" mentioned. Frazier had heard rumors of the former fracas, and had notified Messrs. Mullane, Bralligan, *et al.* that he would have no duelling in his bailiwick; and deep was the mystery surrounding certain consultations held by night in Mullane's quarters.

"The blood of that young braggart be on his own head," said Mullane to his henchmen. "And you, Hodge, can console the disconsolate widow."

He had no more doubt of the issue of the contemplated combat, no more compunction in the matter, than had Thackeray's valiant and inimitable little Gascon, *né* Cabasse, in his duel

with Lord Kew. He had long been the leader of
the Hibernian set, and, despite every effort on the
part of the witnesses to the affray at the sutler's
to keep the matter a secret, rumors got out, and
the Faugh-a-Ballaghs knew their chief had been
braved by that hated coxcomb Winn. Every one
of them knew further that Mullane must have
sent his demand for satisfaction, despite the fact
that his "pistol oi," the right, had been damaged
by the collision and was not yet in condition for
effective service. Everybody who was in the
secret knew that Mr. Winn had instantly accepted, naming Brayton as his second, pistols as
the weapons, and suggesting his father's old duelling set, that had seen long years and some service in the old army, as proper to the occasion;
the time and place, however, would necessarily
depend on the victim of the knock-down blow.
All Winn asked and urged was utter secrecy
meantime.

To Mullane there was nothing in the episode
over which to brood or worry. As dragoon sergeant in the old days, he had "winged his man"
according to the methods described in "Charles
O'Malley" and practised occasionally by his su-
periors in rank. He had known many a bar-room
broil, and was at home with pistol, fists, or sabre,
—no mean antagonist when not unsteadied by

liquor.   He had now a chance of meeting on the
field one of the set he secretly hated, "the snob-
ocracy of the arrumy," and he meant to shoot the
life out of Harry Winn if straight shooting would
do it.   That Winn had taken advantage of him
and knocked him down when he was drunk was
excuse sufficient for the crime he planned; that
he had brought the blow upon himself by an insult ten times more brutal was a matter that concerned him not at all.   He had no wife or child
to worry about: Mrs. Mullane and the various
progeny were old enough to look out for themselves, as indeed most of them had long been ac-
customed to do.   Mullane thirsted for the coming
meeting, and for the prominence its outcome
would give him among all good soldiers all over
Texas.

And as for Winn,—he who had come riding
home from his successful scout barely a fortnight
before, buoyant, hopeful, almost happy,—the
change that had come over him was something all
men saw and none could fully account for.   Cash-
ing the draft from the bank at San Antonio, he
had now enough to take Trott's receipt in full
for the value of the stolen stores, even to some
recovered plunder, slightly damaged by rough
handling and by rain.   He would then still have
some four hundred dollars, and he asked his wife

for certain bills that had been frequently coming to her accompanied by urgent demands. Laura said she had not kept them. Which ought to be paid first? he asked. Which had been longest outstanding? Laura's reply was that she did not know, but if he had got that money from San Antonio at last she ought to have some to send to Madame Chalmette. She positively had not a dinner-dress fit to be seen. Winn did not even glance at the open doors of a big closet, hung thick with costly gowns his wife had hardly worn at all, but that now, she said, were out of style. There were other matters to be thought of than dinner-gowns, he told her, gravely, and her face clouded at once. She had almost forgotten the troubles of the week gone by.

He went down to his den and sat there thinking. What ought he to do? what should he do with this money? Every cent of it would be swallowed up if he squared those commissary accounts and turned the balance into checks and sent it off to pay these bills, and then if Mullane's bullet sped true to its mark, what would there be to take Laura and the baby North? "Home" he dared not say. She had no home: Collabone's diagnosis of that situation was correct. Then, too, if Mullane's pistol did not fail him, there would be no way in which that mysterious friend and beneficiary of his father's could ever be repaid. What right had he to use one cent of this money for any purpose whatever, when another day might be his last? Winn wished he still had the San Antonio check instead of these bulky packages of greenbacks. They were now locked up in Trott's safe, unbroken, pending action at Department Head-Quarters on the new schedule sent thither, based on the recovery of some of the damaged stores. He thought of it all as, long before gun-fire that morning, the black care of his life came and roused him from his fitful sleep and bade him face his daily, hourly torment. He had risen, and as he softly moved about the room, thoughtful for her, she slept on placidly as a happy child, soundly as slept the nurse and the little one in the adjoining room.

Donning his stable dress, he carried his boots into the hall and down the creaking stairs, and sat there, with solitary candle, at his desk, wearily jotting down inexorable figures. The dawn came stealing in the eastward window: from aloft a querulous little wail was uplifted on the stillness of the summer morning. There was no answering hush of loving, motherly voice. Laura could not stand wakeful nights. He tiptoed swiftly up again to rouse the nurse in case she too slept on, but he heard her hand beating drowsy time on the coverlet, and the soothing "Shoo, shoo, shoo," with which she communicated her own heaviness to her little charge. Laura had turned uneasily, he saw as he peeped in at the open doorway, but again slept soundly, her lovely face now full turned towards him, half pillowed on the white and rounded arm he used to kiss with such rapture in the touch of his lips. Her white brow was shaded by the curling wealth of her soft, shining hair. The white eyelids drooped their long curving lashes over the rounded cheeks, faintly tinged with the rosy hue of youth and health. The exquisite lips, warm, delicately moulded, parted just enough to reveal the white, even, pearly teeth. The snowy, rounded throat and neck and shoulders were enhanced in their beauty by the filmy fabric of her gown, beneath which her full bosom slowly rose and fell in healthful respiration. How beautiful she was, how fair a picture of almost girlish innocence and freedom from all worldly dross or care! Even now, in the light of all the gradual revelation of her shallow, selfish vanity, the heart of the man yearned over and softened to her. If he had only realized,—if he had only known more of the world and life and duty other than mere soldier obligation, how different all might have been! What right had he to ask her to be his

wife? She should have wedded a man many years
her senior,—one fitted to guide and direct her,—
able to lavish luxury upon her. It wasn't all her
fault that she had been so thoughtless, poor girl!
What else had her mother been before her?
What else could one expect of her? Would she
miss him? he wondered. Not long,—not long,
thank God! Beauty such as hers would soon win
for her and baby home and comfort such as he
could never give. That was all over. Something
almost like a sob rose from his heart as he bent
and softly touched with his lips the floating curl
above her temple, then turned back to resume his
work and reface his troubles. Thank God, Mullane's pistol would soon end them all and save
him from the sin that was in his soul the day he
took his own revolver with him. She was sleeping still when the morning gun shook the shutter
of her window and he went forth to meet the
sorrows of another day, as he had met those of the
past,—alone.

The air was strangely still, yet the smoke from
the kitchen chimneys back of the barracks settled
downward about the adobe capping or drifted
aimlessly along the roof-trees. Down in the
stream-bed and over about the low bluffs of the
farther shore, swallows and sand-martins were
shooting and slanting about their nests in clamor-

ous, complaining gyration. The flag, run up to
the topmast at the crack of the gun, hung limp
and lifeless, without so much as a flutter. Away
to the northwest, over the pine crests of the range,
a belt of billowy cloud gleamed snow-white at
their summits, but frowned dark and ominous underneath. Huge masses of cumulus, balloon-like,
thrust distended cheeks to the morning kiss of the
sun; but these were well down to the west. The
orient and the zenith skies were fleckless. Over
at the stables two four-mule teams were hitching
in, and army-wagons were being laden with tent-
age, luncheon-baskets, ice, boxes of bottled beer,
band instruments, and the like, all going ahead to
the White Gate, while Frazier's bandsmen were
to follow in another as soon as they had finished
breakfast. Their duty would be to set up the
tents, the dancing-pavilion, and the lunch-tables
on the level green in a lovely dell a mile within
the gates, and have everything in readiness
against the coming of the joyous party from the
post. It was planned to carry the women-folk
and such men as couldn't ride in the available
ambulances and spring wagons, while the cavaliers would canter along on horseback. They
would lunch at one, dance, fish, and flirt through
the afternoon hours, have a supplementary bite
and beer towards five o'clock, and drive home-

ward before dark. "Captain Barclay, as the guest of honor," said Mrs. Frazier, would go with her and 'Manda in her own vehicle, a venerable surrey. The colonel would drive, and Miss Frazier, now withdrawn by a maternal order from the supposed competition, in order that 'Manda's charms might concentrate, was bidden to ride. Winn had no thought of going. Mrs. Frazier had no thought that it would be possible for him or Laura to go,—the latter being reported ill in bed,—and therefore had found it easier to comply with the colonel's dictum that they must be invited, and she did it by dropping in and bidding "Miss Purdy" say to her mistress that she had called to inquire for her, and was so sorry, so very sorry, that her illness would prevent her coming to the picnic, whereupon Laura herself had appeared in becoming *négligée* at the head of the stairs and smilingly assured the nonplussed lady that she was so much better she thought it really might do her good to go. But of this she said no word to Harry until, returning from stables at seven o'clock, he was surprised to find her up and dressing.

On the homeward way he had met Mr. Bralligan, whom he passed without recognition, but not without mental note of the unusual circumstance, Bralligan being a late riser, as a general thing, and having no business at Barclay's quarters anyhow. Brayton awaited him on the piazza and drew his arm within his own.

"Mullane sends word that he'll be ready at sunrise to-morrow, Harry, and I have said we were ready any time."

But the young fellow's voice trembled a bit as he anxiously scanned his classmate's grave, solemn face. It couldn't be that Winn was weakening, losing his nerve. It couldn't be that. But had his trouble so weighed upon him that he really welcomed the possible coming of the end? Brayton's was a hard lot just now. Assiduously he was hiding from his own captain all indications of the forthcoming meeting. Somehow he felt that Barclay would not hesitate to disclose the project to the post commander, and then every cad in Texas would jeer and crow and say it was Winn and he who crawfished. Barclay had noted that Winn seemed avoiding him again, and spoke of it to Brayton, who answered that Winn was avoiding everybody: he was blue and depressed about his affairs.

"Yet I understood that he had received more than enough to settle those commissary accounts," said the captain.

"Oh, yes," answered Brayton, "but there are other matters." How could he tell Barclay that

he thought Winn's love and faith in his wife
were dead and gone? How could he tell him
that Winn would touch no dollar of the money
until he had first met and satisfied another claim?
Barclay's suspicions would have been aroused at
once.

But Winn was having another trouble now.
Laura had set her heart on going to the picnic,
and for no other reason, she declared, than that
she must show the women there was nothing
amiss. If he and she, either or both, should fail
to attend the Fraziers' entertainment, every one
would say he still believed her guilty of having a
rendezvous with Barclay at that unearthly hour,
and that she was unforgiving.

As he had done many a time before, Winn
yielded. What mattered it? There might be
only that day for him. He could accomplish
nothing by absenting himself. He could aid in
brushing away any cloud upon her name by going and being devoted to her. So go they did, and
women who watched with wary and suspicious
eyes long remembered how fond and lover-like
were Winn's attentions to his beautiful wife;
how often on the way he rode to the side of that
ambulance to say some little word to her; how
anxiously he seemed to scan that lowering westward sky, for by the time they reached the Blanca

gorge the cloud-banks were climbing to the zenith and the westward heavens were black as the cinder-patches along the heights about them, where fir and spruce and stunted pine had strewn the slopes with dry, resinous carpet, too easily ignited by the sparks from hunter's pipe or camp-fire. At two o'clock, Blythe, Brooks, and Frazier, clambering a rocky ridge to the southeast of the lovely picnic cove, looked gravely at the blackening sky, then gravely into one another's faces. "I think we ought to start at once," said the colonel. "That's no place to be caught in a storm." And he pointed downward as he spoke.

At their feet was the deep, grassy valley, hemmed by precipitous bluffs. The greensward at the base of the barrier ridge was soft and velvety. A richer soil nourished the roots of the bunch-grass, and all men knew that more than once in bygone days the sudden swelling of the brawling waters that came foaming and swirling down the ravine from the depths of the crested heights within had turned that beautiful little sheltered nook into a deep lake that slowly emptied itself through the narrow, twisting, rocky gorge that ended at the White Gate. On the level turf the dancers were merrily footing it even now to the music of an inspiring quadrille, the pretty gowns of the women, the uniforms of

the men, adding brightness to the picture. Below
the camp the mules and horses were placidly
grazing close by the inner opening of the gorge,
the white covers of the wagons and the snowy
canvas of the two or three tents adding to the
picturesqueness of the scene. All at the feet of
the watching group was life, laughter, and careless joy; all beyond that merry scene a black and
ominous heaven, frowning down on gloomy pine
and rocky hill-side. The ceaseless clamor of the
seething waters, as they turned whirling into the
tortuous gorge, rose steadily above the throb and
thrill of the dance-music, and aloft those relentless clouds sailed sternly eastward over the sky.

Still the smoke from the camp-fires settled back
and shrank about the earth, as though dreading
the encounter with the sleeping forces of the air.
Then, as the watchful eyes of the elders turned
once more up the mountain side, there came a cry
from Brooks. "By God! it's coming! There
isn't a second to lose!"

Frazier, following the direction of that pointing finger, looked upward, saw the crestward firs
and pines and cedars bending, quivering before a
blast as yet unfelt below, saw sheets of ashen
vapor come sailing over the hill-tops and sweeping down the rocky sides, saw the whole mountain face turn black as in a single minute, as

though hiding from the storm that came roaring down the slope, then lighting up the next instant in dazzling, purplish glare, as a zigzag bolt of lightning ripped the storm-cloud in twain, and in the instant, with crash and roar as of a thousand cannon rolled into one, let loose the deluge sleeping in its depths. As though Niagara were suddenly turned upon the hill-side, a vast volume of water swept downward, hissing, foaming, rolling over the rocks, and the leaping spray dashed high in air, as the black wealth of waters came surging down into the ravine.

"A cloud-burst, by all that's holy!" screamed Brooks, as he sprang down the grassy side of the bluff. "Up with you, up the hill-side, for your lives!" The dancers, faltering through the sudden flutter of the band, for the first time looked upward, and saw the peril. Then, men and women, bandsmen and "strikers," the camp made a wild rush up the eastward hill-side. Another blinding flash, another thunderous roar that seemed to shake and loosen the rocks about them, and in that second of brilliant, dazzling glare the watchers could see the white wall of the Blanca come spray-tossing, seething, whirling huge logs and trees on its outermost wave, tumbling them end over end, now deep-engulfed, now high in air,—one immense, furious moving mountain of raging water, sweeping towards them from the depths of the chasm. Then, rolling and frothing over its puny banks in the valley below, a chocolate flood, foam-crested, spread right and left through the deserted camp, licking up the cook-fires, sweeping camp-chairs and tables off their legs, bodily lifting wagons and ambulances and sending them waltzing to the wild music of the storm over the flats where twinkled dainty-slippered feet the moment before, then bore them away towards the inner mouth of the gorge just in time to mix them up with such frantically struggling mules as through native obstinacy had resisted the impulse to scamper to higher ground while yet there was time. Worst sight of all, right there in the midst of the logs, chairs, wagon-beds, that came swirling beneath them, was a despairing woman's struggling form, revealed by a woman's white dress.

"Merciful God!" shrieked Mrs. Faulkner; "it's Laura Winn. She went up towards the falls not ten minutes ago."

Vain fool! What could have been her object? Barclay, never dancing, had been looking smilingly on. Both the Frazier girls had been led, not too willing, away by partners. Four sets had been formed, and Mrs. Winn, pleading fatigue, had asked to be excused, had sauntered past Bar-

clay's seat, and, before his eyes, had turned up
the narrow, winding, sheltered pathway by the
Blanca. Had she dreamed it possible that he
would follow? Follow her he did not. Was
it—a far more charitable thought—in search
of Harry she had gone? Sombre and absent-
minded, he had earlier slipped away among the
trees, avoiding even Brayton. But now Barclay
was seen on the near side of the torrent, limping
up and along the steep slope, in imminent danger
of slipping in, swinging in his hand a long lariat
that he had drawn from the nearest wagon when
the wild up-hill fight began. They remembered
later that he was the last man out of the hollow.
Already Brooks, Brayton, De Lancy, and half a
dozen men were hurrying along the hill-side to
aid, but Brayton reached him first and seized his
arm just as another cry went up from the hill-
top,—just as from the opposite side of the seething torrent the tall figure of Harry Winn came
bounding through the stunted trees, and, hatless,
wild-eyed, he seemed searching the tossing mass
of wreckage on the bosom of the waters. Another instant still a white hand was waved aloft
in their midst ; then a white arm encircling a
log, a terror-stricken white face, all showed dimly
one moment before again borne underneath, hidden by the yellow body of a whirling ambulance,

and in that one instant, far leaping, Winn plunged into the torrent and struck out savagely to reach his wife.

Vain, hopeless effort! Eddying in huge circle at the rocky shoulder just above the entrance to the gorge, the wild waters near the eastward shore bore their burden, jarring and crushing, close under the heights on which were clustered the panic-stricken revellers from Fort Worth. But on the farther side, as it narrowed towards the entrance, the hissing torrent tore like a mill-horse on its way. Into this heaving flood leaped Winn, and, before the eyes of screaming women and helpless, horror-stricken men, was sucked into the rush and whirl of foaming waves sweeping resistless through the rocky cañon, away towards the fair White Gate, away out and beyond the lovely foot-hills, tossed and battered and crushed by whirling logs, dragged under by the branches of uprooted trees, borne away at last, rolling, gasping, still feebly, faintly struggling, until on the broad lowlands the torrent spent the fury of its concentrated spite, and, swiftly still, but no longer raging as when curbed and held by the barrier gate, the Blanca foamed away to strew the tokens of the fearful storm right and left for miles along its banks, and to land all that was mortal of Harry Winn, bruised, battered, yet

so placid in death that strong men's voices broke
when telling how they found him, resting with
weary head upon his arm on the sandy flat
that lay just beneath the little summer-house on
the overhanging bluffs,—just where Laura had
looked down over the misty shallows from that
very height the morning her soldier husband had
reached his home at reveille and found her—
wanting.

They bore her wailing home that night, widowed and crying, Woe is me ! yet with what wild
thoughts throbbing through her brain! Who
was it that came leaping to her aid as she felt herself again dragged under in that swirling eddy?
Whose voice was it that rang upon her drowning
ears? Whose strong arms had clasped and sustained her and held her head above water, while
other strong hands, hauling at the lariat made
fast about his waist, drew them steadily to shore?
Then angels came and ministered to her,—the
women,—while the men clustered about her
dripping hero, Galahad. Only for a moment,
though, for there was mounting bareback in hot
haste and thundering away at mad gallop, despite the drenching rain, for he who had saved
the wife implored those who could ride to haste
and save the husband.

All Fort Worth again went into mourning

with the setting of that woful sun. It had borne
its fill and more of battle and of sudden
death.

And people resurrected Hodge's stories later
on, though Hodge himself was readily excused.
They recalled how Channing's widow and little
ones were cared for after that officer's untimely
death in the shadows of old Laramie Peak. They
recalled Porter's ailing wife and the sea-side
sojourn, and the old ordnance sergeant's family
burned out at Sanders. It wasn't many days before the lovely, drooping widow of poor Harry
Winn was quite well enough to be sent the long
journey to the North; yet some weeks elapsed
before she would consent, she said, to be torn from
her beloved's grave. When, gently as possible,
she was told in July that the quarters she still
occupied were needed for her husband's successor,
she proposed to spend a few weeks with Mr. and
Mrs. Faulkner, but they were forced to limit that
visit to a few days. There was no reason why she
could not have started in June, for that devoted
mother, Mrs. Waite, had dropped temporarily the
pursuit of Senators and Representatives in Congress assembled, and wired that she would meet
her daughter in New Orleans, and the commanding general at San Antonio notified her that
abundant means for all her homeward journey-

ing for self and nurse and baby were in his hands.
She thought she ought to stay until all poor
Harry's affairs were straightened out; and Frazier had to say that that, too, was all attended to.
Yet all the while she seemed to think that she
could not sufficiently thank the heroic Captain
Barclay, and begged to see him for that purpose,
also to consult him, day after day, until—was
there collusion?—he suddenly received orders to
proceed to San Antonio on court-martial duty,
and was on his way before she knew it,—before,
said the Fraziers, she could get ready to go with
him. Nor was he there when she passed through,
under Fuller's escort, to the Gulf, nor did she see
him once again in Texas. Letters, fervently
grateful letters, came to him from Washington,
whither she had flitted, and where, it is reported,
she was to have a clerkship. But when people
spoke of her to Barclay he smiled gravely and
had nothing to say. All her late husband's accounts were declared settled and closed within a
very few months, and all men knew by that time
whose hand it was that had lifted the burden;
yet Laura Waite had lost the last vestige of her
power where Galbraith Barclay was concerned.

Long before the fall set in, Barclay returned
to his post of duty, eagerly welcomed by officers
and men, except the Faugh-a-Ballaghs. Some-

body had sent from San Antonio a marble head-
stone for Winn's lonely grave in the little ceme-
tery. Somebody had secured for his widow that
clerkship in the Treasury Department, which
within another year she left to wed a veteran ad-
mirer of her mother, to the unappeasable wrath
of that well-preserved matron and the secret joy
of 'Manda Frazier, who thought that now perhaps
the eyes of Galahad would open to her own many
charms of mind and person. Yet they did not.
Somebody in a childish, sprawling hand was
writing letters every week to the doughboy
trooper, who by that time had the best drilled
company at Worth, owing, said the Faugh-a-
Ballaghs, when forced to admit the fact, to Brayton's abilities and to an Irish sergeant. Barclay's
weekly mail was bigger than that of anybody else
except the commanding officer, whose missives,
however, were mainly official, and the number of
letters penned in feminine or childish hands
seemed, like Galahad's godchildren, ever on the
increase. Mrs. Blythe came back from leave,
bonnier than ever, and blissful beyond compare
in the possession of secrets she could not share
with even her oldest cronies, yet that leaked out
in ways no man could hope to stop. Ned Lawrence's children were well, happy, thriving,—
little Jim at Barclay's home with other godsons,

two or three, where a widowed sister cared for
them as for her own, so said Mrs. Blythe when
fairly cornered, while Ada was at a famous old
Connecticut school not far from the Barclay
homestead.

"Good heavens!" said Blythe, one day in late
October, "these women have powers of divination
that would be priceless at police head-quarters.
Why, they've got hold of facts I thought only
Mrs. Blythe and I knew,—facts that Barclay
would have kept concealed from every one, but
that we simply can't deny."

And so, little by little, the details of some, at
least, of Galahad's benefactions became known,
though no man knew how many more were held
in reserve. For three long years he lived his
simple, studious, dutiful life at Worth, a man
the soldiers and their wives and children learned
to love and look up to as their model of all that
was kind and humane (they well-nigh worshipped
him at Christmas times),—a man his brother officers of the better class honored as friend and
comrade, worth their whole trust and esteem, and
from the armor of whose reserve and tolerance
the shafts of the envious and malicious glanced
harmless into empty air.

There were women, old and young, who
thought him lacking in more ways than one. The

Fraziers said not much, but looked unutterable things when they went North on leave and people asked for Galahad. It was a family tradition that he had treated 'Manda very badly; that is, mamma said as much, but the elder sister had views of her own not entirely in harmony with those of her beloved parent. 'Manda herself found consolation by marrying in the army not two years later, and her husband thinks to this very day that Barclay, with all his wealth, secretly envies him his treasure, though admitting, in those lucid intervals to which so many lords are subject, that perhaps Barclay wasn't so confoundedly unlucky after all. It was at their quarters some years later still, at a far-distant post, that in the course of an evening's call, in company with his host, Lieutenant-Colonel Brooks, the chronicler of a portion, at least, of this episode of old-time army life was favored with the most important facts of all.

"What do you think!" said the stout possessor of Mrs. 'Manda's matured and rounded charms, as he came bustling in with the *Army and Navy* in his hand, "Galahad Barclay's married at last. Here it is : To Ada, only daughter of the late Brevet Lieutenant-Colonel Lawrence, —th U. S. Cavalry."

"Ada Lawrence! That child!" screamed

madame, with eyes and drawl expansive. "Well, of all——"

But others, who have seen her in her happy wifehood, declare that Ada Lawrence grew up to be one of the loveliest of the lovely girls that married in the army,—and they are legion.

THE END.

By A. Conan Doyle.

A Desert Drama.

BEING THE TRAGEDY OF THE KOROSKO. With thirty-two full-page illustrations. 12mo. Cloth, ornamental, $1.50.

"The author has a splendid chance to use his descriptive powers and splendid material to draw contrasts in nationalities and to compare civilization with barbarity. This he has done very successfully, and the 'Desert Drama' forms an interesting narrative. Besides his splendid description of the desert and his portraiture of the cruel Dervishes and their fierce religious zeal, the author has given each of his characters a distinctiveness which is marked out very cleverly."—*Philadelphia Evening Telegraph.*

"Full of excitement and passing from one crisis to another with true dramatic force. The author has been inexorable, too, for a novelist of his usually amiable predilections. He started out to tell a tragic tale, and he adheres to his purpose, two of his travellers losing their lives in the bitter misfortune befalling the party that comes up the Nile through Nubia so gayly and so fearlessly. The happiness of the people on the Korosko is turned to woe of the most terrifying description, just how we leave the reader to find out for himself, only noting that Dr. Doyle has struck out on a line comparatively new for him in this book, and that he has treated it with no diminution of his skill as a narrator. The book is readable from beginning to end."—*New York Tribune.*

"With the opening paragraph, the reader's interest is awakened, to remain and to gain in attentiveness with the progress and development of the plot to the final chapter. A novel in which the imagination of its author is observed to broaden out and to search for incident beyond ordinary fields of discovery, and yet to adorn the narrative it weaves with a staying interest that is both living and timely—such a novel possesses not a little of the spirit of the busy, purposeful days in which we live, and contains virility enough and striking motif, sufficient to render it at once and lastingly popular. Those qualities Dr. Doyle's latest novel has in a telling degree. It is thoroughly a novel of to-day, full of interest, spirited, thrilling, and bright with the most vivid of pictures for the surpassing pleasure both of the traveler and the stay-at-home. The author has evidently visited the places of which he so fluently and pleasurably writes, and has been a participator in some stirring desert scenes, or he surely could not have written so acceptably of them as he does in the present tale."—*Boston Courier.*

J. B. LIPPINCOTT COMPANY, PHILADELPHIA.

By Florence Belknap Gilmour.

TRANSLATED FROM THE FRENCH OF
LÉON DE TINSEAU.
12mo.   Cloth, $1.00 per volume.

In Quest of the Ideal.

"It possesses distinct interest, and there are not a few passages which command our deepest feelings."—*Philadelphia Evening Bulletin.*

"This story owes much of its charm to the skill of the translator, Florence Belknap Gilmour, who has translated several other of this author's books, and who has been able to catch his style in a way rarely met with.   The characters are carefully and naturally drawn, and there is a great deal of dialogue which is bright."—*Boston Times.*

"The story has a strong, uplifting tone throughout, and the seriousness and the crusading spirit of these modern seekers for the ideal, is shared by every individual in the novel, as well as by the reader.   The translator reproduces the original with a master knowledge.   Her choice of words is smooth and easy, and they convey exactly the meaning the author meant they should."—*Boston Courier.*

A Forgotten Debt.

"The story reads as if it were a true life tale, told simply and with none of the unpleasant element found repulsive to American taste in many of the latest French novels.   It is healthful and hearty, and well suited for summer's day perusal by old or young."—*Boston Transcript.*

"A very interesting novel which tells of life in the French provinces and metropolis, and also in an American frontier military post, and depicts the local atmosphere of all three—a difficult feat, which shows the versatility and analytical and descriptive powers of the author.   The plot is interesting, and holds the attention of the reader from beginning to end."—*Detroit Tribune.*

J. B. LIPPINCOTT COMPANY, PHILADELPHIA.

By Edgar Fawcett.

A Romance of Old New York.

Small 12mo. Yellow cloth, ornamental, with polished yellow edges, $1.00.

Douglas Duane.

Square 12mo. Paper, 50 cents; cloth, $1.00.

A Demoralizing Marriage.

Square 12mo. Paper, 50 cents; cloth, $1.00.

By W. C. Morrow.

The Ape, the Idiot, and Other People.

12mo. Ornamentally bound, deckle edges, $1.25.

J. B. LIPPINCOTT COMPANY, PHILADELPHIA.

By Rachel Penn.

[Mrs. E. S. Willard.]

A Son of Israel.

12mo. Cloth, $1.25.

" The picture of the Russian ghetto impresses us, like Zangwill's own sketches, with its seemingly truthful realism. And delightful creations, truly, are the little dark-eyed dancer, Salome, and her family, and the ancient La Meldola. The interior of Michael's household gives us an excellent view of Russian family life. In fact, exceptional praise is due the author, who is said to be the wife of Edwin S. Willard, the actor."—*The Philadelphia Record.*

" Rachel Penn need have no fears about allowing her work to stand upon its merits. ' A Son of Israel' is a powerful and fascinating contribution to current fiction having a deep religious coloring, of which ' Quo Vadis' and ' Fabius the Roman' are notable examples The scene of the story is laid in Russia, and its predominating theme is the bitter hostility of the Russian nobility toward the much despised Jew. David Rheba, a skilled silversmith, is the central figure, and his strong yet pure and simple Christian character is drawn with wonderful clearness."—*The Minneapolis Tribune.*

" ' A Son of Israel; an Original Story,' by Rachel Penn, has a dangerous title, for original stories were never common, and are now scarcer than ever, but the characterization is justified by the contents. It is as odd a tale as will often be seen."—*Springfield Republican.*

" It is an open secret that Rachel Penn, whose first serious venture in fiction, ' A Son of Israel,' is in reality the wife of Mr. E. S. Willard, the well-known English actor. Mrs. Willard was formerly an actress, and, like her husband, began her career under the auspices of the late E. A. Sothern, of Lord Dundreary fame. After playing opposite rôles for several seasons, the two were married, Mrs. Willard retiring soon afterwards from the stage. As she has no children to occupy her thoughts, and lacks the physique to endure the strain of accompanying her husband on his lengthy tours in the United States and elsewhere, Mrs. Willard has for several years devoted much time to literary work."—*New York Commercial Advertiser.*

" Fine dramatic qualities mark ' A Son of Israel,' which is not to be wondered at when we learn that the supposed author is Mrs. E. S. Willard, wife of the actor, using the pseudonym Rachel Penn. The writer has abandoned the commonplace in devising a plot, and shows literary skill as well as spirit and vivacity in the narration."—*Philadelphia Press.*

" The story fairly bristles with melodrama, and contains incident enough for any three ordinary books, while a complete list of the *dramatis personæ*, which range all the way from an ex-ballet dancer to a buyer for an English firm of dealers in curios, and from serfs to the Czarowitz himself, would tax the limits of the longest handbill."—*New York Commercial Advertiser.*

" ' A Son of Israel' is a timely book. Of peculiar interest now, the book will be read, appreciated, and condemned. It is a novel of feeling, a novel built out of the suffering sympathy of a woman's heart for the oppressed of her people and of her God."—*Chattanooga Times.*

J. B. LIPPINCOTT COMPANY, PHILADELPHIA.

By S. Baring-Gould.

Richard Cable, the Lightshipman.

12mo.   Cloth, $1.00.

The Queen of Love.

12mo.   Paper, 50 cents; cloth, $1.00.

The Gaverocks.

12mo.   Cloth, $1.00.

Court Royal : A Story of Cross-Currents.

12mo.   Cloth, $1.00.

Guavas the Tinner.

12mo.   Illustrated.   Paper, 50 cents; cloth, $1.00.

"There is a kind of flavor about this book which alone elevates it far above the ordinary novel, quite apart from any particular merit in the story. The curious aloofness of these miners from the generality of English people, and the convincing manner in which the author throws the reader amongst them and makes them perfectly natural, perhaps account for this flavor of plausible singularity; but it is a hard task to define it.   The story itself has a grandeur in harmony with the wild and rugged scenery which is its setting. Isolt, with her cold and passionate nature, is a most haunting figure, and her mysterious appearances are very dramatic. The hero in a different way is equally fine,—distinguished by a silence at once pathetic and magnificent."—*London Athenæum.*

J. B. LIPPINCOTT COMPANY, PHILADELPHIA.